I0534301

THE LAUGHTER IN THE WOODS

ALEXANDER ENGEL-HODGKINSON

THE LAUGHTER IN THE WOODS

1st paperback edition ISBN #978-1-989331-23-1
1st Kindle edition ISBN #978-0-9952174-7-8
1st Kobo edition ISBN #978-1-989331-28-6
Cover artwork by Alexander Engel-Hodgkinson

Published by
Dark Brothers Incorporated

2

PARENTAL ADVISORY

This book contains some gruesome violent content, strong profanity, some sexual material, and disturbing themes intended for mature readers aged 17 and up.

AUTHOR'S COMMENT

I've been putting this one off for a bit too long, now. Seven years! Wow! But I think the time I spent working over the concept was beneficial. Better late than never, right?

CHAPTERS

THE LAUGHTER IN THE WOODS

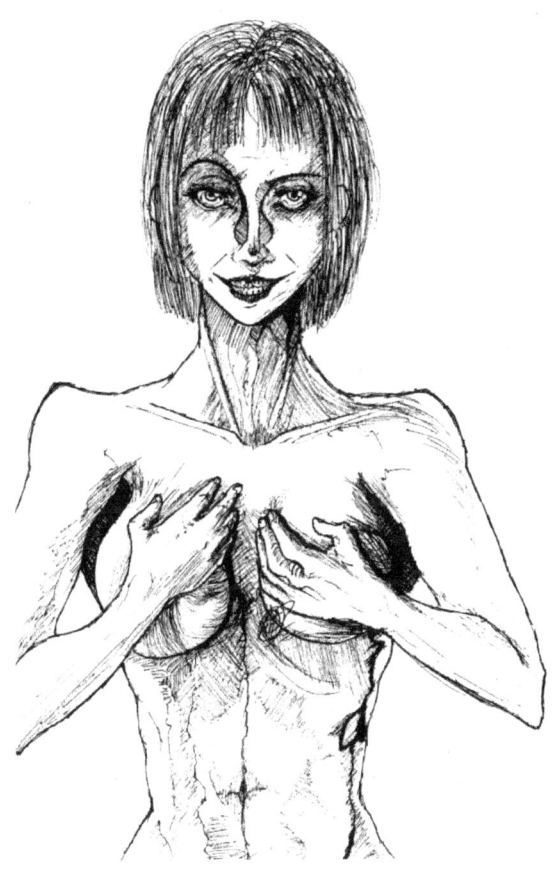

Friday, December 15th, 2000 - Part I

It was once a man. Its blackened, misshapen husk shambled through the trees. Snow and frozen leaves crunched under its lopsided feet. Its forearms bowed outward, charred flesh clinging stubbornly to bone. In the night, it was a vague outline on an indefinite journey, its destination unknown even to itself. As the sun ascended, rose-coloured rays streaking through the trees and turned the snow pink, the thing's joints stiffened and its posture curved forward, head pivoting slightly.

"Dust," it said, and then it stopped moving entirely. It wouldn't start moving again until next nightfall.

*

A frosty glaze of snow-covered trees stabbed their jagged branches into the grey winter sky. A foot of Styrofoam-white blanketed the ground. Tire treads cut muddy swaths along the lonely backroad that split a thin straight line between the wooded areas.

The minivan travelling that road was

6

probably the fifth to set its tires on it today. To the birds flying above, it probably looked like a cherry red dot against a vast backdrop of white and grey.

The Carmichaels were on their way to grandma's house. Jack sat behind the wheel, hazel eyes watching for any deer through aviator sunglasses. His wife, Cassandra Carmichael, stared out the passenger window beside him while their three boys—Harry, five; Martin, seven; and Alistair, eight—sat quietly in the back with their twin cousins, ten-year-olds Brian and Hannah Lansbergh-Carmichael. The kids were quiet only because they were reading their books, playing their portable video games, texting on their phones, or in Martin's case, staring blankly at the back of his father's seat with music blaring through his headset from a Walkman cassette player.

Jack glanced in the rearview mirror at his passengers, then looked at his wife, the only passenger who wasn't distracted by a manmade device. "Honey?"

"Hm?" She turned her beautiful arctic blue eyes to him.

He cocked his head back. She looked

7

into the back and smiled. "So what? They're quiet."

"Ridiculous," he said. "Absolutely ridiculous."

"You're too old-fashioned for your own good, Jackie boy."

"Yeah?" Jack said. "If being 'old-fashioned' means keeping my brain from getting fried by a dozen digital screens, then consider me a famous figure from ancient history who hated technology."

"Ted Kaczynski," Hannah said.

Jack peered at her in the rearview mirror. "Who?"

"The Unabomber."

Jack shook his head. "I'm not *that* radical. I watch TV like any other guy. I like my sports. I like my beer. I like my beer combined with my sports. And pizza. But I have responsibilities. Just like *you* and your brother have responsibilities. And my kids have responsibilities. For you guys, it's simple. Just the odd chore, here and there. You even get paid for it." He looked at the road for a few seconds, then his eyes flicked back to the mirror to see Hannah tapping on her cell phone again, no longer engaged in the conversation, if he

8

could even call it that. He wanted to throw it out the window. He said to his wife, "If the world ended in the next minute, I don't think they'd notice. Except the eavesdropper with selective hearing."

Cassandra giggled and looked back out the window.

The boulder at the end of the driveway was just up ahead. If it weren't for that boulder, Jack would have driven by the house without even realizing it on numerous occasions. *Thank Christ for boulders, eh?*

"Here we are," he said to no one in particular as he pulled into the driveway. Despite the packed-down snow, the familiar crunch of gravel was still there; it pulled the kids' attention away from their devices to the house ahead.

A few cars were already parked in the wide gravel driveway outside of the two-car garage. Attached to that garage was grandma's house—a humble masterpiece in classic red brick structuring. Tiled windows lined the wall in narrow slits and a sandstone path curved around its front entrance, leading from the driveway to the patio and garden in back. The living room's window was much taller and wider than any other window in the house, culminating to a bulbous crown at the top. The generously decorated Christmas tree stood framed within, glimmering brilliantly in a glorious multi-coloured radiance. The black tiled roof divided into a series of hips and valleys; half of the roof above the living room was a skylight with diamond-patterned tiles. The eavestroughs were all decorated with Christmas lights.

"Alright, kids," Jack announced, preparing himself. "Put your things away." He watched them in the rearview as they stuffed their phones and games in their pockets, and wanted to laugh. He just knew that was what they'd do. "Your mechanical masters stay in the van."

An inevitable wave of protests flooded the back seat. Jack raised his voice over them, not quite shouting, "Alright, alright! No arguments, okay? Phones and games and headphones stay in the van and that's the last time I'm gonna say it."

"That's so stupid!" Hannah exclaimed.

"It's not stupid. It's a social gathering between friends and family," Jack

10

said patiently. "When I was your age, I didn't even *have* a phone."

Alistair said, "Weren't phones just invented then?"

"Haha," Jack said sarcastically, "you're so funny, Al. So funny. You're also wrong, and you're something else, too. Can you guess what else you are?"

"What?"

Jack smiled. "You're leaving your phone in the van."

Another wave of protests. Harry pouted and Martin whined. Hannah heaved an exaggerated growling sigh as she rolled her eyes and said, "This sucks! You're the worst uncle ever!"

"I'm also in charge, young lady." Jack's smile evolved into an ear-to-ear grin. "Your parents will no doubt thank me for separating you from your electronic overlords. We haven't seen grandma since Thanksgiving; the least you can do is talk to someone face to face." He parked between a white Subaru Leone and a blue Chevrolet Astro. "I see Deb and Marcy beat us here," he remarked. "Makes me wonder why we drove Marcy's kids if she was gonna be here sooner."

11

"She was helping your mom, and their dad's picking up Marcus from the hospital."

"Why would John pick up Marcus?"

"John has a truck. Can't exactly fit the wheelchair in her Subaru, Jack."

"How come I'm always the last to know about these things?"

"I told you last night."

"No, you didn't."

"*Yes*, actually, I did. You just weren't listening. Again. And remember—be nice." Cassandra placed a patient hand on his shoulder. "Let's not get off to a bad start already. It's Christmas."

"I'm being nice," he said curtly, snapping the car into park. "Really."

Hannah got out first and made a brisk start for the garage.

Jack rolled down his window and called out, "Hannah!"

Hannah stomped her foot down and turned around, huffing. "*What*?"

"Phone."

Hannah returned and shoved her phone into the pocket in the back of Jack's seat. "You're the worst!"

"Sticks and stones, kiddo."

12

The boys muttered under their breath as they left their phones and games on the seats and stepped out of the van, being sure to slam the doors behind them. Martin was the last to leave, keeping his headphones around his neck.

"Same rules apply, Martin." Jack got out of the van and pulled the back door open. "Toss 'em in."

"But dad..."

"No 'buts.' In."

"I won't wear it, I swear."

"Martin, you're already wearing them," Jack said sternly. "I won't ask again."

With a heavy sigh, Martin took them off and handed them to his father, who placed the headphones around the gear stick. Jack patted his son's head, shutting the door to the van as he did so. "Good man. Go say hi to grandma."

As Martin ran to the house, Jack joined his wife in a slow walk to the door. He noticed her look and breathed a sigh of his own. "I know. I know exactly what you're gonna say."

"You're too strict sometimes, Jackie."

"There it is. Hon, I've said it

13

before—"

"'Spare the rod, spoil the child,' yes, yes, so you've said."

"And will continue to say."

"Don't you think that maybe you're a little *too* stern, though?"

"Maybe the odd time, here and there."

They reached the garage door next to the shutters. Harry and Alistair had already taken turns ringing the doorbell. Hannah was pouting with her arms folded across her chest off to one side. Brian and Alistair stood a few paces away from the rest of the group, looking down the trail extending from the driveway into the forest behind the house. The trees seemed to arch over the path, their branches bending, their trunks curving, forming a round tunnel that extended farther than they could see. They knew that the path led to the clearing where the toolshed and the small Quonset hut were. Grandpa's four-wheeler and tractor were inside. They fondly remembered when he helped them trap a squirrel in a cage from that toolshed. The toolshed and the hut held many things, not all of which they'd seen. Kids weren't allowed in either structure.

14

The breeze whistled and tittered through wooden chimes dangling above the children's little heads. Their high notes reached piercing frequencies, attracting Alistair's attention from the path. Smooth pine tubes clacked together on silver strings. Another bundle of chimes answered their call in the forest where Alistair couldn't see them. They sounded like half a dozen train horns howling in the distance.

The door opened, and a beaming old lady as tall as she was blonde greeted the children with open arms, a welcoming smile, and the gentlest blue eyes. She looked thin and frail, but she carried herself like she wasn't. "Hello! You made it!"

The children greeted their grandmother affectionately, each one stopping to embrace her warmly before they went to take their boots off in the foyer. Jack followed them in with his wife and hugged his mother, secretly admiring her sleek black BMW E34 parked beside the stairs, the overhead lights gleaming brightly on its surface. "Hi, Mom."

"Jackie, how've you been? Staying in shape?"

"You know it."

"Know it?" She raised an eyebrow, maintaining a jokingly stern look as she looked him over. "You're getting a belly!"

"And you're as skinny as ever, you old hag," Jack fired back, grinning from ear to ear.

"Stop it, you two," Cassandra chided them playfully. "You're no better than the little fiends we dragged along." She traded little greeting kisses on both cheeks with her mother-in-law. "Merry Christmas, Mrs. Carmichael."

"Oh, please, I've told you a thousand times, Cassandra—call me Wilma."

"It feels wrong, somehow, like I'm disrespecting my elders."

"Elders, *ha*," Wilma chuckled as she shut the garage door and followed them up the steps into the foyer. "I'm as young and spry as ever. Long drive?"

"The road conditions weren't so bad," Jack said.

"Good to hear. I saw snow coming down last night and got a little worried."

The grandfather clock in the living room sang its Westminster chimes, announcing the half-hour to all who were

16

present to hear it. Wilma went straight into the kitchen to continue dinner preparations.

Lounge music played quietly on the surround sound system. It was a new feature for Jack. Deb and Marcy were seated at the table next to a large picture window that overlooked the back deck and the garden beyond. Two middle-aged women, Deb being Dan Jr's wife; Marcy, Jack and Dan Jr's older sister, chatted over glasses of sparkling red wine. They barely acknowledged the newcomers until Jack was practically leaning over them. They looked up at him, their mouths straight lines. "Yes?" Marcy asked.

"Can we help you?" Deb added, swishing back a few locks of hazelnut hair.

"Where's Dan?"

"In the house somewhere."

"Really?"

"Yeah, but it's weird hearing you refer to Dad by his first name."

"I meant the other one, smartass."

"Just got off work," Deb said impatiently. "He should be here soon with Marcus."

Marcy asked, "How were the kids?"

"Your kids died on the way here,"

17

Jack said with an exaggerated shrug. "Sorry. We had to throw them overboard or else the entire car would've sunk into the snow. It was your kids or mine, and I kinda like mine, so…" He chuckled.

Both women smirked mirthlessly at his joke.

"Tough crowd." Jack went to pour himself a drink. He muttered to Cassandra, who beat him to the counter with a stack of dishes in her hands, "This is gonna be a fun night."

She shook her head. A woman needed to possess the patience of angels to put up with Jack.

Wilma was watching the children as they played in the living room in front of the stone fireplace and the Christmas tree. They marveled excitedly over the stacks of wrapped presents under it. She started setting the table in the dining room next to the buffet and hutch filled with real, intricately patterned china dishes on display. Cassandra brought her stack of plates over. "Here, I'll help you with the table-setting, Wilma."

"Oh, you don't need to do that."

"I like helping. Don't worry about a

18

thing."

Jack filled his glass with red wine and sidled up to his mother. "Where's Dad?"

"Basement." She sounded none-too-pleased. "He's been spending a lotta time down there lately. See if you can get his butt up here, will ya?"

"Sure thing, Ma." Jack went through the kitchen again, passing his sister and sister-in-law, into the foyer. He stumbled over boots and coats that had fallen off their hooks to the door, in which was a large rectangular window. He opened the door and went down the steps onto the garage's cold concrete floor. The fridge and freezer box in the corner hummed loudly by the door to the outside. He turned and walked alongside Wilma's BMW to the back of the garage to a door at the end. He opened it and peered down a flight of stairs into the dimly lit basement. "Dad?" He heard things being moved around, but there was no verbal reply. "Dad?"

"That you, Jackie boy?"

"It's me. Mom wants you to, and I quote, 'get your butt upstairs.'"

"I'm a little busy at the moment. Could—could you give me a hand,

19

actually?"

Jack started down the stairs, shutting the door behind him. The wooden planks creaked in protest under his feet. As he descended, the clutter of his father's work area became visible. A pile of videotapes seemed to have spilled out of one of his two shelving units along the far wall. A desk against the wall and a work table in the middle of the basement were piled high with papers, a television set and VCR, newspapers, an envelope with 'TO WHOM IT MAY CONCERN' scrawled on it in black permanent marker, and other things that Jack didn't bother looking at. An unused pool table stood collecting dust on the other side of the basement next to some equally dusty filing cabinets and boxes full of miscellaneous things. His father's deer hunting things were locked in a glass case by the toilet stall. A camouflage jacket and matching cap hung above a bolt-action rifle and a magnum revolver; boxes of ammunition were stored near them. Set against the wall behind the stairs was a bank of televisions stacked on each other in four rows of five. Extension cords and power bars were spooled in a thick,

20

entangled bushel on the floor to the left of it. Live surveillance feeds of the surrounding property were shown on each screen in soft, grainy quality. There were no cameras pointed at the house, as far as Jack could see.

His father was standing in the middle of the work area, having somehow navigated through all the chaos his lack of organization had created. He sat down on a stool, eyes glued to the TV on his desk, his back facing his son. Jack couldn't make out the fuzzy picture on the small screen.

"What're you doing down here?" Jack asked, touching down on the concrete floor. He stopped outside of the work area.

His father, Dan Snr, swiveled on his stool and tossed a black rectangular object into his son's hands. "Look at this."

Jack caught it and exclaimed with mock wonder and excitement: "Wow, a videotape! I've never seen one of these before."

"Gimme that." Dan Snr lurched over the work table and snatched it back. "Smartass. I know you know what it is." He held it up. "Look at the label."

Jack looked. "What label?"

21

"Look closer." Dan Snr tossed it to him again.

Jack caught it and studied it with a keener eye. He spotted faint scratches on the plastic where a label had once been. He also noticed patches of white adhesive where the label had been torn off without delicacy. He still wasn't the least bit interested, but he figured he'd humour the old man for a few minutes. "Okay. I give up. What am I looking at?"

"A conspiracy. A cover-up. Do you see the letters etched into the plastic? Whoever wrote on these labels was very aggressive, I think. They tore off the labels, but they couldn't tear off the scratch marks."

"Think so?" Jack could see some scratches, but they were too scarce to make any words out of them. He ran his finger over it and felt a thin layer of grime cling to it. He rubbed it on his thumb, grimacing in disgust.

"I still have a few friends in the department." Dan Snr turned back to the static on the TV. "The Chief wanted me to have a look at some of this stuff."

"This is crime scene stuff? You mean

22

this *isn't* your porn collection?"

"Don't be ridiculous. I don't need porn when your mother is still alive and *very* much in excellent health and shape."

"Gross."

"Some of it is from a crime scene. Some of what survived the fire, anyway. The rest was saved from a fire pit just a few houses down the road in a backyard. The homeowner ran off with his kid a few years ago. Jameson thinks he went to BC, or maybe he went to the States or something. Can't say. Somebody was trying to cover something up, or so some of the boys seem to think."

"What do you think?"

"Still too early to tell what I think. I just got this stuff yesterday. Jameson gave me a week to sort it out, give him my thoughts."

"Why? There a shortage of brains at the station?"

"He just wanted my perspective on a case that seemed to've gone cold till last autumn, when a pattern began to emerge. Come look at this. Come, come."

Suddenly interested, Jack decided to step over papers and garbage to his father's

23

side. Dan Snr was rewinding the tape with his remote control. Jack saw nothing but static snow the whole time, even when Dan Snr pushed play and let it proceed normally. Jack gave him the benefit of the doubt and watched the screen for a short while, but as it went on, his patience thinned out. "What're we looking at?"

"Don't you see it?"

"See what? The snow?"

"Look closer."

"Getting tired of you saying that."

"There's a face in the snow."

Jack glanced at his father. The old man was engrossed in whatever he was seeing that Jack couldn't. He started to wonder if many people grow senile in their early seventies. He figured it wasn't too uncommon. He placed the tape down on the envelope, 'TO WHOM IT MAY CONCERN'. "I think it's time we went upstairs, Dad."

"Whatsamatter? Spooked?"

"Nah. Mom's getting impatient. You know how she gets during the festive season."

Dan Snr sighed. "Yeah, yeah, I know how she gets. Go on up. Tell her I'll be

24

there in a minute."

"Alright. I'll let her know you'll be up soon. Very soon. Shortly. A few minutes at most."

"Yup." Dan Snr was nodding his head, still staring at the TV. "I won't be long. Just wrapping something up."

Jack gave him a doubtful glance from the foot of the stairs, feeling strangely about his father's new hobby. "Make it quick, eh, Dad?"

"That's what I said." Dan Snr hadn't turned around.

Jack squinted at the bank of surveillance feeds just beyond the stairway railing, then went upstairs.

Friday, December 15th, 2000 - Part II

Jack entered the kitchen and saw that Marcy sat alone. He joined his sister at the table, glancing at a squirrel hopping around Deb on the back deck as he sat down. She was leaning against the rail, staring out at the frozen pond, seemingly unbothered by the cold snow that touched her bare feet. She was only wearing a coat over her casual clothes. "Is she crazy? What's she doing out there?" he asked.

"Trying to get hypothermia's my guess. She's been acting weird lately."

"Dad's acting weird, too."

"Dad's always been weird," Marcy replied, sipping her wine. Jack noticed it was fuller than before.

"I just mean weirder."

Marcy shook her head slightly. "Dad's *always* been weird, Jack."

"I know. But this is weirder. Weirder than usual."

"Whatever you say."

Before Jack could respond, Wilma called out to him from the dining room.

26

"Where's your dad?"

"He said he'll be up in a minute."

She gave him a doubtful smirk and then continued chatting with Cassandra.

"How're the kids?" Marcy asked. She sounded uninterested.

"Kids're just fine," he answered. "How's the wine?"

"Red." She sipped it. "Bitter."

"How's John?" Deb still hadn't moved from her spot on the deck. She hadn't moved at all. Not a muscle on her body shivered visibly from the cold. "Averages about forty below this time of night," he added quietly.

"He's fine. Got a new job at the lumberyard."

"Nice." He looked away from the window at his sister. "Long hours?"

"Yeah. Too long, I think."

"Money's gotta be good, right?"

"What good's the money if we don't have the time or energy to spend it?" She looked very tired now, glaring at him with half-open eyes.

"Good point. Maybe that's why he does it."

"To spend as much time away from

27

me as possible?"

"Now how would you come up with such an absurd conclusion?" He gave her a wry smirk to show that he was joking, and she returned the expression to show she was in on it.

"Because I know men, and how they think."

"It's another woman."

"Oh, please."

"Or maybe he just really likes trees."

"More than his wife?"

Jack shrugged exaggeratedly. "There are no limits to a man's depravity."

"Some of Dad's wisdom?"

"I agree with the sentiment."

"Slow your roll. John's anything but depraved. A little dense, maybe." She drank to that, a long sip.

"I noticed."

"But certainly not depraved." She set the glass down. Jack noticed a glimmer of darkness in her humourless expression. "Occupied, maybe."

"Occupied?"

She did a little dismissive wave with her free hand, the fingers on her right hand still tightly gripping the stem of her wine

28

glass. "Nah, that's the wrong word to use."

"Okay, then."

"Man, I could use a smoke, but I can't find my lighter anywhere."

"Forgot it at home?"

"I was sure I brought it."

"The car?"

"Nope. I checked."

The kids were getting rowdy and hadn't heard their grandmother tell them to quiet down. "Excuse me." Jack stood up and went into the living room to intervene. "Did you hear your grandma? Simmer down." He noticed that Alistair and Martin were missing and turned left, went by the second entrance to the kitchen behind the counter. He passed the antique grandfather clock standing by the hallway entrance; on the other side was the front door that no one ever used, which faced the road. He entered the hallway. The bathroom was on the left, the guest room further down on the right across from the master bedroom; the laundry room was at the very end of the hall between them. He barely glanced into the laundry room as he turned into the guest room to catch Alistair and Martin playing on a Gameboy Advance. They were perched on the end of the water bed, their swinging feet nearly hitting the dresser that ran the entire width of the room, on which was set a panoramic mirror. The snow was bright white through the tall rectangular window behind them. Another mirror, as tall and narrow as the window, leaned against the wall beside the door.

"We go through this every year, boys." Jack sighed, leaning against the doorframe. Before they could protest, he said tersely, "Put the game back in the drawer, and go join your relatives in the living room."

"But Dad!"

"Come on, Dad, they're *boring*!"

Jack rebuked them with a stern look.

The boys heaved exaggerated sighs as they got off the bed. Alistair turned off the Gameboy, tossed it back in the drawer, and shoved it shut with his knee. They each received a moderate smack on the ass as they filed out of the room. Jack followed them down the hall and parted from them as they joined their cousins and youngest brother in front of the fireplace. He went over to the dining room where his wife stood and kissed her cheek, making her

30

smile. "Anything I can do?"

"Just make sure the kids stay outta trouble," she said.

"Already on it."

"Then sit there and look pretty while your mother and I put the finishing touches on the table setting."

He saluted her and went to rejoin his sister at the window table when Wilma took gentle hold of his sleeve. "You told your father I miss him, right?"

"Yeah," he said, and stole a glance toward the foyer, "just taking his sweet time getting up here."

As if on cue, the front door opened, and Dan Snr shambled in, noisily stumbling over the kids' boots and snow pants. "Ah! Jeez."

It was like the kids all had their own radar—one of them shouted, "Grandpa!" and they all came running through the kitchen to crowd him in the little foyer.

"Heeyyy!" he shouted, arms outstretched. "One at a time now. One at a time! Jeez. Act like you never had a grandpa before." He took turns hugging them all and then allowed them to drag him into the kitchen, where Wilma awaited him

31

with arms folded across her chest.

"And where have *you* been?" she asked him.

"You know, baby." He kissed her lips and flashed his most charming smile in her direction. "Work stuff."

"Mhmm. Work stuff. You should be up here, talking to your kids and grandkids."

"I know, I'm sorry, hon. I'm just really swamped."

"You can be swamped tomorrow. How important can it be you have to be on it all the time during Christmas?"

"There's just a lot to sort through, and not a whole helluva lotta time to sort through it."

She grunted with disapproval.

He continued his explanation, as if he were on trial in front of a judge. "This case has been going for years, now. Almost half a decade! Can you believe it? There's too much going on that they've outsourced it to me. They're desperate, Wilma. Too many people've died already, including our neighbours across the woods—"

"Quiet down," she snapped. Then, more gently, "You're scaring the kids."

32

"I'm not scared," Hannah said. "In fact, I find it fascinating. I'm watching lots of documentaries about, like, crime and stuff."

"Yeah," Alistair chimed in, "what're you looking at, Grandpa? Can I see?"

"I want to see, too!" Martin exclaimed.

"Hey, me, too," Brian said. "I'm not scared of anything."

Hannah continued, "I saw this one documentary about this guy named Ed Gein. He was a serial killer, in case you didn't know who he was."

"Oh, yeah?" Dan Snr replied to her. "All about the serial killers now, are ya?"

"Oh," Marcy groaned from the table, "she's just *enthralled* with them. Might have to take an ax to the TV before she turns into one."

Dan Snr laughed. He asked his granddaughter, "Ever heard of Albert Fish?"

Hannah made a face. "No. Who's he?"

Wilma glared at Dan Snr, who didn't even have to look at her to know that he would be banished to the doghouse if he

33

said anything more. Jack stepped in before the head of the family could chastise her husband further. "Nobody's seein' anything. All of you, be gone—back into the living room from whence you came, foul demons!"

The kids giggled and screeched, stampeding out of the kitchen around their grandparents.

"And stop running in the house," Cassandra said, raising her voice above their racket. She turned on the TV set by the tree and gave Alistair the remote. "Change it to something sensible, please." To the rest of them: "All of you will sit here and keep the noise levels down to a minimum until dinner. Is that understood?" She nodded with approval in the midst of all the "Yes, Mom," and "Yes, Aunt Cass," replies she was receiving. "Good."

Martin asked, "Can I play the Gameboy?"

"No, you always fight over it."

She rejoined the other adults in the kitchen. Jack had taken his seat across the table from Marcy, and Wilma and Dan Snr were working together behind the counter putting the final touches on dinner. The

34

smell of turkey, honeyed ham, steamed vegetables, and mashed potatoes was very strong, now. Cassandra's mouth watered from the aromas that surrounded her.

Westminster chimes filled the house. The gong followed, striking five times. The grandfather clock fell silent afterwards.

Something bothered her. She noticed movement in the corner of her eye and turned to follow it, saw Deb striding across the ankle-deep blanket of snow on the deck. "Why's Deb outside without her boots?"

Wilma looked up suddenly from her food preparations behind the counter. "She's *what*?" She peered through the window at Deb, who seemed to be preoccupied with something in the greying skies above. "Good Lord, somebody bring her in here and ask her what her malfunction is. It's thirty below out there!"

Dan Snr lifted the glass lid off a pot of steaming vegetables and took in the steam with a pleasant smile on his face without acknowledging his daughter-in-law outside. "Mmmm."

Jack grabbed his boots from the foyer and carried them through the kitchen to the door next to the table.

"Thank you, honey," Cassandra said with a sweet smile as he passed her. "You should put on your coat, too."

"Shouldn't be that long." He kissed her, slipped into his boots, stepped out onto the deck. "Deb?" His breath plumed in front of his face. The cold hit him like a brick wall. A shiver ran through his body.

Deb didn't seem to hear him, craning her neck with her eyes staring beyond the treeline.

"Deb," he said, approaching her. "What're you doing out here?"

She pirouetted on the ball of her left foot, arms at her sides.

"Deb!" Jack had raised his voice. It startled even him, echoing in the woods around them. Deb stopped twirling and stared at him with a blank expression on her face.

"Why're you yelling, Jackie boy?"

"What's the matter with you? I called you three times."

"Oh. I guess I spaced out."

"Guess so. Come inside; my mom's getting worried about you running around out here barefoot. I thought women got cold easier than men?"

36

"Usually the case." She shrugged. "It never bothered me."

"Come on inside."

"Is dinner ready?"

"Just about."

"Are John and Marcus here yet?"

"Not yet."

She made a face.

"Mom's getting worried, though. What do you say we ease her worries at least a little? You know how old ladies get."

"Alright." Her fingers made squiggly little trails in the snow lining the deck's rails as she made her way to the kitchen's door.

"What were you looking at, anyway?"

"Just admiring nature, that's all."

"I see." Jack glanced into the vast expanse of forest beyond the backyard. Sensing movement, his eyes flitted right, where the pond and garden was. He saw nothing but various shades of grey and brown splotching the whiteness of winter. The forest was silent and still. Rabbits didn't roam. Birds made no sounds. No breeze whistled through the wooden chimes dangling between thick, sparkling icicles from the gutter guards.

He followed Deb inside.

Cassandra had a towel and told Deb to sit where Jack had been sitting so she could wipe her feet dry.

"No, no, don't," Deb protested, "it's fine. I'll do it." She took the towel and stooped down to dry her feet.

Cassandra cast a worried glance at her husband as he shut the door behind him. She shivered from the last rush of cold air, so he shed his coat and draped it around her shoulders. She gave him an appreciative smile, but the worry remained clear on her face.

Marcy hadn't moved from her spot beside the door. "Jesus, Jackie, you let all the warm air out."

Jack ignored her. "Where's Dad?"

Wilma looked around, almost startled by the subtlety of her husband's exit. Then her expression hardened. "Probably downstairs. Again."

"Want me to get him?"

She shook her head and sighed. "Leave him. Dinner won't be ready for at least another forty minutes, anyway."

"Okay."

38

"What could be so important?" Cassandra asked.

Wilma shook her head again. "He's really in deep with this one. Getting him to come upstairs at a decent time is like trying to dig out termites with a butter knife. It's like he's obsessed."

Jack felt the need to offer a more comforting thought. "It's not the first time he's gotten bogged down on a case before, Mom."

"Not like this."

"Sure he has."

"Jackie, there hasn't been a case quite like this around here. We moved up here to get away from the noise and the hustle and bustle of the city. Now it's like we never left. Can you check on him?"

"He just left. I'm sure he's fine." But his mother's eyes told him that hollow reassurances wouldn't be enough. "Fine. I'll go check on him."

"Thank you."

Jack and Cassandra exchanged glances from across the room that only the two of them could understand. Then he looked around and asked, "Anybody want a beer or something from the fridge? Since

39

I'm going out to the garage anyway."

Marcy held up her wine. "I'm good."

Deb grabbed the bottle and swished it around. "Still a good amount of wine left."

Cassandra said, "I'll ask the kids if they want some pop."

Jack shook his head no. "They're hyper enough as it is."

"Jack…"

"Can we at least hold them off till dinnertime?"

She sighed. "Fine."

"You want anything?"

"No."

"Alright." Jack left, throwing his boots toward the coat rack in the foyer as he passed through to the garage. He circled back around in the garage to the basement door. He opened it. "Dad?" Like last time, there was no response. He could hear the high-pitched frequencies emitted from his father's television sets. He descended to the floor, looking over at his father's cluttered workspace as soon as his head cleared the ceiling trusses.

Dan Snr had planted himself firmly in front of the TV, his wrinkled old face hovering inches from the flickering screen.

40

Jack couldn't tell whether or not the tape he was watching had any picture on it, or if it was just more static snow.

"Anything good on?" he asked his father.

Dan Snr didn't acknowledge him. Without turning away from the screen, he reached to a shelf on his left and retrieved an envelope. He tore it open and rifled through the papers. Jack didn't see him lower his head to see what he was doing. It was as if the old man was doing it all by feel. Finally, he pulled out a document and held it up to the TV screen's light.

"Dust." The sound of his voice gave Jack a mild start.

"What's that, Dad?"

"Just sorting through the facts, son. Sorting through all these facts."

"Mom's getting irritated, Dad."

"Is dinner ready yet?"

"Not yet."

"Then why're you down here, disrupting my work?"

"I—"

"This is important work," Dan Snr grunted. "Somebody's gotta figure it out soon. Why shouldn't it be me?"

"How long have you been down here today?"

"Today? Since I woke up this morning."

"Mom wants to see you."

"She's been up my ass all day, son. Do your old man a favour and tell her I'll be there when dinner's ready." He turned the document ninety degrees to the left. His head tilted with it. "Not a minute sooner. Okay?"

Jack felt a pang of resentment rising. "Since when did you talk about Mom like that?"

"I'm curt with you because I love you. All of you. Haven't you heard the rumours? The strange shit that's been going on around here these past few years? Forgive me if I don't wanna be social while something like this sleeps below our feet."

"Sleeps?"

"Yes, son. *Sleeps.*"

Jack approached the work table. The envelope with 'TO WHOM IT MAY CONCERN' written on it caught his eye from under the videotape without a label. "What do you mean, 'sleeps'?"

"I mean just that. Is it dark yet?"

42

"Almost."

"Is Junior here yet?"

"Shouldn't be too much longer before he's here with Marcus and John."

"Good."

"Why do you ask?"

"Because I'm starving."

Jack took another look around the basement. He saw the glass case with his father's hunting things in it. The revolver was gone. "Dad, where's the revolver?"

"Hm?" Dan Snr turned on his stool. "What'd you say?"

"Did you notice that the revolver's not in the gun case?"

"Of course. I have it right here." He pointed at a shadowy spot beside the TV. "They're never going to see it coming."

"*Who*, Dad?"

"The cultists, son. And whatever they trapped on these films. Check the surveillance feeds. See anything out there?"

Without bothering to look at the stack of televisions behind him, Jack tossed his hands helplessly and started back up the stairs. He heard Dan Snr call up to him, "Let me know when dinner's ready, will

43

ya?"

"It's hopeless," Jack told his mother when he returned to the kitchen. "He's hopeless. Stubborn old bastard refuses to come up until dinner's ready."

"Whatever," she said as she pulled the turkey out of the oven. She set it down in the center of the kitchen table, between Deb and Marcy, and placed a lid over it. "I have half a mind not to call him up at all with the way he's been lately."

"That looks delicious," Deb said. "Smells so good!"

"Mhm," Wilma grunted.

Jack followed his mother behind the counter. "He said something about a cult."

Wilma grabbed a stick of butter from the fridge and slapped it on a glass saucer. "I don't really care what he said if it involves that stupid investigation. It's not healthy. As soon as he's up, he's downstairs. Then he's there until one in the morning. Sometimes four. Back at it again at six or seven. He hardly sleeps anymore."

Marcy threw in her two cents from her spot at the table: "It's not like he hasn't done this before."

"He hasn't," Wilma replied, "not like

44

this. This is different."

"How?" Jack asked.

"I don't know. Different. He's obsessed with it. There was the obsession with previous investigations, and then there's this. Whatever this is, this is *not* normal."

Deb was staring out the window. "John's late."

Marcy checked her wrist watch. "Not for another half-hour at the most, Deb."

Jack turned. "What time is it?"

Westminster chimes from the grandfather clock rang from the living room in response to Jack's question. Five-thirty.

"That was perfectly timed," Marcy said.

"It was," Jack agreed.

"They're not coming in," Deb said.

"What's that supposed to mean?" Cassandra made a little laugh. She'd pulled out a chair at the other table and was now sitting in it. She glanced over at the kids. They were quietly watching TV. She turned back to the adults in the kitchen. "Of course they're coming in."

Jack and Wilma were staring at Deb with visible concern. Deb was still peering through the window at the forest behind the garden. The snow was shimmering hot pink and red, reflecting the sunset. The trees, crystalized pillars of ice and snow, created slanted walls of shadow across the backyard.

"You okay, Deb?" Jack took a step toward her. "You're acting weird."

"Yeah." Marcy sipped her wine, finishing the glass. "You used to get cold."

"I'm fine."

"You don't sound fine. You on drugs, Deb?"

"Jack," Cassandra said.

Marcy added, "I was gonna ask if you had bad circulation in your feet and just couldn't feel it anymore. Jeez, Jack. You think so?"

Jack shrugged to his wife, faltering under the daggers her eyes were shooting at him. "I thought it was a valid question."

"That's rude," said Cassandra.

"She's usually bubbly and high-spirited. None of this... standing-out-in-minus-forty-five-without-boots melancholy bullshit she's got going on here."

"*Jack*," Cassandra snapped.

"What?"

46

"You're not helping."

"I'm fine." Deb turned her head, flashed them all a pretty little smile. "Really. I'm just tired, that's all. And starving. When's dinner? I'm tempted to reach under this lid and steal the turkey all for myself."

"The food's almost ready," Wilma said. "Patience is supposed to be a virtue."

"It's a virtue I don't really have today," Deb replied. She took the wine bottle and refilled her glass. Offered it to Marcy. "More wine?"

"Not till dinner. Thanks."

"Save some for the rest of us," Jack said.

"And for those who haven't arrived yet," Cassandra added. "I'm sure John or Junior would love some."

"Oh, them again." Deb gave a blasé shrug and poured the blood-red liquid into her glass. "They won't miss it."

*

The sun's last rays twinkled between the tree branches, and then it sank below the horizon. Pink, orange, and red clouds swirled against the encroaching darkness of night seeping across the sky like an oil spill.

47

The forest was static. No birds chirped. No raccoons or rabbits or deer bounded through the frosted shrubberies. The ice turned blue and the trees turned black as night blanketed the treetops.

A mound of snow trembled and fell away from the husk as *it* stirred. The maggots on its face were stuck to its dried, shriveled flesh by the relentless cold.

"Dust," it said, and then it began to walk again.

Friday, December 15th, 2000 - Part III

An hour passed. The grandfather clock sang its usual tune for the middle of the sixth hour of the evening. John, Dan Jnr, and Marcus still hadn't arrived. The children, impatient from smelling the food and not tasting it ever since they got there, had started asking questions.

"Is the food ready yet?"

"When's dinner ready?"

"Can we eat yet?"

"Dad, I'm starving! When can we eat?"

Jack and his wife exchanged looks. Jack said, "I don't see why not. It's getting cold."

The kids cheered.

Marcy raised her hand. "Hold up. We're starting without them?"

Wilma was quick to jump to Jack's defense. "I didn't toil away all day just for it to get cold. Besides, there's no reason we can't save the boys some for later. There's plenty to go around for seconds and thirds."

"But Mom!" Marcy protested.

49

"No 'buts,' this is my house and the boys knew what time was best to show up. That's no reason for the children not to eat anything. It's past six."

"Grab a plate," Jack told them as he and Cassandra prepared the living room table for a buffet-style roundabout. "Grab what you can eat. Martin, don't go overboard, or I'll eat your share of dessert." With a playful wink at his middle child, he added, "You don't wanna miss out on pumpkin pie, right?"

Martin shook his head from behind his raised plate.

"Whipped cream and ice cream?"

Martin shook his head again.

"And," Jack continued, "I want you all to fill at least a third of your plates with vegetables."

The only child to not groan was Alistair. Hannah smirked. "You're not my dad, Uncle Jack."

"Hannah," Marcy called out in a warning tone, "Do what your uncle tells you."

Hannah turned to see Jack returning her smug look in spades, his mocking eyes shaded by the overhead chandelier.

50

Frowning, defeated, she dumped a spoonful of steamed mixed vegetables on her plate and moved along around the table.

After the children filled their plates, Jack said to them, "So long as you guys promise not to make a huge mess, you can eat your dinner in the living room, okay? Your uncles will be here soon. Go back to the TV, now."

Cassandra asked them, "Who wants soda?"

Jack suppressed a tired sigh as the kids asked for a variety of brands. Cassandra went to the garage to retrieve them from the little fridge. She came back with cans of pop on a platter for the children.

"I'm gonna call John, see what's taking him so long." Marcy got up and went into the dining room. The landline was cradled on the wall by the second kitchen entrance, beside the antique longcase clock. She dialed John's cell phone number. After three rings, an answering machine picked up. "Damn it." She hung up and tried again, and was dismayed when she got the same result. She cradled the receiver and swore.

Cassandra looked over at her. "No answer?"

"Answering machine."

"Better than no service."

"Doesn't make much of a difference. He's not answering either way. Mom, what's Junior's number?"

"Check my address book. It's, uh... hold on." Wilma stooped down and pulled out a drawer beside the stove. She lifted her address book and flicked through the pages to 'C' section and ran her finger down the third page to Dan Jnr's number and home address. She handed it to Marcy. "Third page, seventh line down."

Holding the receiver between her ear and shoulder, Marcy found the number and dialed Dan Jnr's cell phone number. Waited, impatiently tapping her foot. "No answer." She jabbed the hook switch and tried again. "Straight to voicemail this time."

Cassandra asked, "Does Marcus have a phone?"

Deb said, "No. Didn't think he'd need one till he was in high school."

"So they're a little late," Jack said, munching on a turkey leg. "No big deal.

52

Probably driving slowly because of the roads."

"Guys… what if they slipped off the roads?" Marcy was clutching the phone so tightly that her knuckles had turned white.

"Jesus," Jack exclaimed, "that's a little extreme, don't you think? They're not even half an hour behind schedule yet. I'm telling you, they're just being cautious on those roads."

"They're not," Deb said.

"Yeah and how would *you* know?" Marcy asked her from behind the counter, agitation edging her voice. "You think you can see the future?"

"I can't see the future," Deb answered. "I just know they're not coming."

"That's not funny, Deb," Marcy said. "If you know something, stop messing around and tell me. Did they say anything about any other stops? Detours? Possible delays?"

"No." Deb raised the wine bottle. Only a third of its contents remained. "Since they won't be coming in, I propose we finish the wine. A toast to the rest of us."

53

"What's your problem?" Marcy asked. "Seriously. Your son and your husband are unaccounted for and you're acting like it's no big deal."

"They're just late," Jack said, showing his free palm and a turkey leg in the other hand in a gesture of surrender. "Let's not spin this into something out of control. You two're being ridiculous. Do you act like this every time John or Dan are a few minutes late?"

"Weather aside," Marcy said, "John is never late."

"Aside? Or *permitting*?" Jack turned his palm and turkey leg up. "The roads weren't great when Cassandra and I brought the kids. Now that the sun's down, visibility is worse. I don't think they got into an accident. I've seen both of them drive. They aren't reckless drivers. They'd slow down a bit, right? Marcy, you'd know that John doesn't drive like he's gunning for NASCAR. And Dan doesn't drive like a moron, either. They'll get here. Just give them a little while longer. And hell." He chuckled. "They probably stopped at a gas station because Marcus had to pee. You know how difficult that can be sometimes,

54

what with the lack of feeling in his legs and uh... his attitude, sometimes. No disrespect intended, I think he's a good kid, but sometimes it can take twenty, thirty minutes just to get him on the toilet and off again."

"All good points. However, even if that were the case," Marcy said, "it's not even snowing right now. It shouldn't take them this long. John was supposed to get off work at 4:30 today."

"Maybe he was asked to stay later?"

"Then why wouldn't he call? Why wouldn't he answer his phone?"

Jack shrugged. "Beats me. Maybe his phone's dead."

"He knows the number to this house. I-it's not like the lumberyard doesn't have any phones around."

"I dunno what else to tell you, sis, except that there's probably a good reason why they haven't shown up yet, or called ahead. Maybe they forgot to charge their phones or something."

"So far that's all speculation."

"That's all I can give you. It's probably nothing, anyway. So relax."

"And if it's *not* nothing?"

"If they're not here in the next two or

three hours, *then* we can start entertaining the idea that something went wrong. But I can almost guarantee you that they'll be here in the next hour, at least. Then we'll all have to make fun of you for making a big deal out of nothing."

Cassandra cut in: "No, we won't, because that's mean, right, Jackie?"

"Sure," he said, frowning. "Mean." He shrugged apologetically to his wife. She was not amused.

Wilma said, "I'm sure they're just fine, sweetie. The only *real* no-show to this party is my husband."

They all shared a small, somewhat uneasy laugh. The tension still remained. No one could push the possibility completely out of their minds. What if Marcy was right? What if Deb somehow knew something terrible had happened? Jack wondered if he was right about the guarantee he'd made, or if he was just pulling it out of his ass.

Against his better judgment, Jack said, "Everything is going to be fine." He bit into his turkey leg and ripped a chunk of dark meat off the bone with his teeth. Chewing graciously, he added, "Really."

56

Cassandra, having returned next to him with an empty tray, elbowed him none-too-gently in the ribs. "You're not helping, hon."

"Just trying to lighten the mood. It's a party, right?"

"There's someone in the garden," Deb said.

Everyone turned and saw that she was staring vacantly through the window. They gathered around her, followed her gaze through the frosted glass at the figure in shadow standing just behind the pond, partially obscured by the trees and snow-covered shrubs. Tall and slender, almost inhumanly thin, with no features that any of them could make out from their vantage point. The sun's light was fading fast. The figure stood almost entirely in shadow, even as the solar pathway lights flicked on under the blanket of snow.

"Who the hell is that?" Jack asked.

"Probably one of the neighbours' kids," Marcy suggested.

"No," Wilma replied from over Deb's right shoulder, "that doesn't look like their children. I can't tell who that is…"

Jack went back into the foyer, slipped

into his boots, and returned to the kitchen. He stepped past the group and opened the door.

Cassandra grabbed his arm. "What're you doing, Jack?"

"Just asking him what his problem is."

"Don't..."

"It'll be fine. Promise." He stepped out of her reach onto the deck and followed the rail toward the garden. His eyes were fixed on the figure. It stood perfectly still beyond the pond's frozen surface. Snow crunched under Jack's boots as he slowly approached. Something about the figure didn't seem right, didn't seem *natural*. The way it stood, or the way its head seemed to be tilted slightly to the left as it watched him.

"Who goes there?" he called out.

The figure didn't move or reply.

Jack glanced at his family members behind the window. Deb was watching him with an unusual intensity he'd never seen on her face in the entire thirteen or fourteen years he'd known her. All the other faces hovering around her appeared concerned or at the very least, interested.

He turned back around and took a few more steps until he'd reached the step over the patio, where the flagstone path winding into the garden began. At this closer distance, his luck hadn't improved; the intruder's features couldn't be made out. It was as if the man standing in the woods was a walking shadow, blacker than night.

"Who are you?" he asked him. "This is private property, buddy. You know what that means?"

The figure didn't reply.

"Means you're trespassing. Now, I suggest you leave before we call the cops. Alright? It's Christmas. I'm trying to be nice, here, you know? My wife's been on my ass about being nice."

The figure didn't move.

Jack heaved a sigh. His breath plumed whitely in front of his face. "I'm starting to lose my patience with you, just a little bit." He stepped off the deck and followed the solar pathway lights toward the pond.

"Jack!" Cassandra yelled from the kitchen doorway. "Don't get close to him! He could be dangerous."

Jack hadn't taken his eyes off of the

figure. "Nah. What's a scrawny guy like this gonna do to me?" He took another step.

The figure disappeared behind the brush and scampered back into the woods, giggling with childlike glee.

"Hey!" Jack yelled, startled, and went after him.

"Jack!" Cassandra shouted. "Jack, leave him alone!"

Jack could hear twigs snapping and ice breaking under the fleeing intruder's feet. He passed the pond, kicking a pathway light out by accident. He threw the shrubs aside and peered into the woods, squinting, trying to see something where the pathway lights couldn't reach. He could hear the figure running, and then the running suddenly stopped, the last notes of their weird laugh hanging in the air.

Jack froze. He listened. He heard the wind chimes whistling from the driveway. He heard the breeze whisper softly in the trees. He heard Cassandra and Wilma calling him. He couldn't see anything, not even the lights that usually turned on around the toolshed and the small Quonset hut when the sun went down at the end of the path. He was surrounded by towering black outlines and deep blue hillocks of snow and frosted underbrush.

Unwilling to venture further, Jack turned back. He returned to the safety of the pathway lights and checked the door on the patio that led into the back of the garage. It was locked. He went around the garage, out of his family's sight, and tried to lift each of the shutters. He couldn't. The sound of packed snow crunching under his boots was almost deafening in his ears. He glanced at the trio of vehicles parked by the path's entrance. Nothing moved there, nor did it make a sound.

The two front doors would likely be unlocked. He opened the garage door parallel to the foyer steps, stuck his arm in, turned the latch on the doorknob, and shut it behind him. Now there were just the two *actual* front doors that no one ever used: one to the laundry room and the main one by the living room around the corner. A chill wind sent an unpleasant tingle down his spine. Jack shivered and hugged himself. Followed the lights around the side of the house and paused at the turn to assess the trees gathered close together between the house and the ditch along the roadside. He squinted, scanning the still scene. It was eerily tranquil out here.

He saw a small, grey cloud roll out from behind a tree and started toward it. Snow squeaked under the rubber soles of his boots. "Who goes there?"

A shape blurred noisily from behind the tree and streaked across the front lawn, shrieking with psychotic joy. The sound paralyzed Jack where he stood. He watched the trespasser flee into the darker part of the woods, listening to the echo assault his ears with the overlapping sounds of a child screaming in terror, a woman howling with uncontrollable grief, a man roaring with immeasurable rage.

It disappeared, its demented laughter lingering in the trees.

Jack hadn't realized he'd been holding his breath. He exhaled shakily and tested the French doors that provided entry to the laundry room. They rattled, locked. He ran to the door in the alcove above the front step, hoping it was unlocked so that he could retreat into the house's safe walls.

It was also locked.

"Shit," he hissed. Turning, he peered

62

out of the alcove, searching the front lawn for the trespasser. He went back to the door and banged on it. The laughter seemed to ring over and over in his ears. His knees felt like they'd give out under his weight. He banged on the door again. "Let me in, goddamn it!"

A latch turned. Hannah threw open the door, looking pale. "Uncle Jack?"

Jack shoved his way in and slammed the door shut, locked it, and then peered through the rectangular window into the trees again.

"What's wrong, Uncle Jack?" Brian asked.

The kids all began to gather. They were quickly joined by the adults.

"Why were you outside, Dad?" Alistair asked.

"Just looking around," Jack said, not wanting to frighten them with the truth. Not until he had to.

"Can *I* play outside?" Harry asked.

"Fuck no you can't," Jack said.

"Language, Jack," Cassandra said. "Back to the TV, kids." One look in Jack's eyes told her all she needed to know. She broke eye contact to regard the children

63

with a gentler tone of voice. "Go on, now. Everything's alright."

"Why were you outside, Dad?" Alistair asked.

"Didn't you hear your mother?" Marcy gave him a light smack on the behind. "Go watch the TV."

"Fine!" Alistair went to pout with the other mystified kids on the living room floor.

"Jack?"

Jack looked at each of their faces in turn—Wilma, Marcy, and Cassandra. Deb was still in the kitchen, or at least not here.

Jack panted heavily, finding it difficult to speak. He fell against the door and slid to the floor.

"No, no, you don't." Cassandra stooped down and slung his left arm over her shoulder. She grunted as she dragged him to his feet. "Up you get."

Wilma offered to put on some hot chocolate. Cassandra and Marcy helped Jack into a chair beside Deb at the table.

"That was stupid and reckless, my love," Cassandra said.

"Who was that out there?" Marcy asked.

64

"Here, sweetie." Wilma lowered a mug of hot chocolate into Jack's trembling hands. Jack glanced down at the three marshmallows melting into its rich brown surface. "It's hot," she warned him. She called out, "Any of you kids want hot chocolate?" A wave of high-pitched cheers for hot chocolate came back from the living room, many of them asking for marshmallows, *all* the marshmallows.

"F-first pop, now hot chocolate with marshmallows." Jack sighed deeply. "Open Pandora's Box, why don't you?"

"Who was it, Jack?" Marcy asked.

"I don't know. I didn't get a good enough look."

"Stupid." Cassandra shook her head. "That was so stupid, Jack, running into the woods like that after them."

"I didn't run far," he replied. "They were too fast. Visibility's shit out there. I didn't have a flashlight or a weapon with me. But I made sure the doors were locked."

"For God's sake, Jack," Marcy huffed, "who the hell would be out there this time of night?"

"I don't know," he answered.

65

"Somebody with a weird sense of humour, I guess."

"You look like you saw a ghost. Did you shit yourself, too?"

"Very funny. No. I don't think it was a ghost. Just an asshole. Or two assholes. There was another one out front. Couldn't have been the same one."

"Could've been Dan and John playing pranks." Marcy shrugged. She was out of ideas for a best-case scenario now.

"Nah." Jack blew on his hot chocolate. His hands were still shaking. "Nah, it wasn't them. Whoever it was, it wasn't them."

"How can you be so sure?" Cassandra asked.

"They sounded nothing like John or Junior."

"You're saying 'they' like you know for a fact it's more than one," Marcy said.

"No way could it've been the same person out front. The first guy lost me in the forest behind the house, running in the opposite direction. And the guy hanging around the front was there awhile. Had to've been. I didn't see any footprints."

"What's that supposed to mean?"

66

"Have you seen any snow coming down, Marcy? Either he can jump farther than anyone you or I know, or he was camping up in the trees or something. I don't know. All I know is that there weren't any damn footprints. That snow was smooth until he ran off."

While Cassandra tried to console her husband with her arms around his shoulders, Marcy cast a worried glance toward her mother.

Wilma, leaning against the edge of the counter, said, "I think I'll call the police."

"Why bother?" Jack asked. "They're gone, now."

"They might come back."

"*If* they come back, yeah, let's call the cops," Jack said, "but I think I scared those jokers off. They've had their fun."

"No," Deb said from her spot by the window, "they'll be back."

"And *you* can be quiet. I've had it up to here with you."

"Jack," Cassandra snapped, "Please. It's not her fault. She's just weird tonight."

"Yeah. Weird." Frowning, Jack sipped his hot chocolate.

Marcy said, "There could be more of them. You said the snow wasn't touched around the guy out front, right? So what you're saying is that there could be more of them out there. Hiding out." She rubbed her temples with trembling fingers. "Jesus, it's like we're under siege by some real dedicated maniacs."

Jack scoffed. "We're not under siege. That's ridiculous. It was a couple of dumb kids."

"How many kids are *that* tall?" Marcy fired back.

Jack shrugged. "Basketball players?"

"You're impossible. This is why I only talk to you three times a year."

"Four."

"Whatever."

Cassandra said, "This really isn't the time for this…"

"Agreed," Wilma said, grabbing the phone and dialing a number.

"Who're you calling?" Jack asked.

"Bethany, next door." She waited, a troubled look on her face. Then she hung up. "No answer."

"What'd you want to call Bethany for?"

68

"Just wanted to see if she heard anything, but I guess she's asleep, or out with friends."

"Want me to go over there and check?" Jack asked.

"No. No, it's fine." Wilma's concern wasn't as easily concealed as she'd hoped.

"What about the other neighbours?" Marcy suggested. "They could've heard something."

Wilma tried the other house. "Not in service. That's strange." She shook her head in exasperation. "I just spoke with her last night."

Jack doubled down on his offer. "Look, I could drive out there right now and start knocking on doors."

"No, I really don't think that's necessary. Anyone up for seconds?"

"You haven't even had firsts yet, Ma," Jack replied.

"Oh! Of course." Wilma went to the table and grabbed a plate. With a pair of tongs in her other hand, she asked jokingly, "Which dish did I burn the least?"

"The turkey," Jack said. "Leave that all for me. No one else likes it but me."

Wilma shot him with a knowing

smirk.

"Don't listen to this fool," Cassandra lightly shoved him out of his mother's way as she filled her plate. "You cooked it all to perfection."

Marcy concurred with positive murmurs, her mouth too full of food to form words.

As soon as Wilma filled her plate, the children went into an uproar in front of the window. "They're here!"

Friday, December 15th, 2000 - Part IV

Brian shouted from the living room, "They're here! Uncle Dan and Dad are here!"

Cassandra turned to see the kids gathered around the tree, looking through the large window behind it at the truck jouncing up the driveway.

"See?" Jack said, grinning from ear to ear. "What'd I say? Huh? What'd I say?"

Marcy smiled with relief and started for the door.

Deb bolted, knocking over the chair she was sitting on. She disappeared into the foyer and threw open the door to the garage. She was a startling blur.

"Deb?" Jack called after her. He and Marcy followed Deb. They reached the stairs in the garage just as Deb had thrown herself into the path of the incoming pickup truck.

"Debbie!" Marcy screamed.

The truck swerved to avoid her, plowed into Deb's Chevrolet Astro. Its entire right side flew upwards, sheering off

71

the Astro's roof as it twirled in a lazy arc, passing Deb who stood giggling with the wine bottle in one hand and something else in the other. She watched it fly. Snow and gravel was flung from its tires in every direction. It smashed onto Jack and Marcy's cars, crumpling in their roofs, and toppled off of them on its side. Gasoline spewed from the gash in its tank.

"Oh, my God!" Marcy threw her hands up over her mouth, eyes bulging in horror.

"Jesus! Holy shit!" Jack shouted, staring at the wrecked pickup in shock.

Deb hooted with laughter, gleeful like a child playing a game. "They saw me! They saw me!" A small flame appeared in her hand. Marcy's lighter traced a wiggling yellow line through the darkness above her head as she ran toward the wreckage.

"Deb! What the hell're you doing?" Jack took off after her, running full-tilt. "Deb!"

Marcy watched helplessly from the doorway. It all seemed so surreal…

Deb hurled the lighter into the truck's pooling gasoline, igniting it. Even when the flames caught, she was still running

72

toward it.

The flames caused Jack to skid to a clumsy stop. "Deb! Stop! Deb! *Deeeeb*!"

The fire spread to the other cars. Deb hopscotched right into the burning circle and danced madly around in it, dousing herself with the last of the wine. Flames crawled up her legs and swelled around her blouse and then consumed her. She howled with laughter, still dancing until the roar of the pickup truck exploding overpowered her. She vanished in the gout of fire that stabbed into the night sky.

Jack shielded his face from the blinding flash, the blast of heat. Marcy shrieked and raced toward the wreckage. "John! Dan! Marcus! *JOOHHNN*!"

A figure engulfed in angry flames crawled out of the back of the pickup's cab. Its guttural cries echoed through the forest. It no longer sounded human. Jack couldn't tell which one it was. Junior? John? Marcus? The flames were too bright, and the figure was totally engulfed. Jack sprang up and jumped to the flailing man. "Roll on the snow!" he yelled at the burning man as he scooped handfuls of snow and gravel onto him in a frantic, semicircular motion.

73

"Roll! Roll! Jesus, please, *roll on the snow!*"

The figure had stopped screaming. He stretched his arm out and dropped to the ground with an unmistakable finality. Jack refused to accept it. He yelled at his sister to keep throwing snow on him. No use. She was hysterical.

Then the Subaru violently exploded behind the pickup, belching a bright red mushroom cloud over their heads. The heatwave slammed them to the drive. Jack rolled to his feet and shoved Marcy away from the flames. The inferno snarled, flicking its tongues after them hungrily. Jack shoved her away. She was still screaming, trying to push him off of her.

Dan Snr seemingly appeared from out of nowhere. He helped Jack drag Marcy away from the flaming wreckage. Jack's minivan blew apart. The three family members tumbled to the ground again. Marcy wriggled free and scrambled for the pickup. Jack leaped after her and tackled her to the ground. "They're dead!" he shouted, parrying her wildly swinging arms and blinking as her fists battered against his head. "You can't—stop! You can't do

74

anything for them now! Marcy!"

"Let me go! I can still—there's still a chance! Get the fuck off of me!"

"They're gone!" He slammed her shoulders and wrists to the frozen gravel. Most of the fight in her seemed to dissipate. "They're gone! Do you understand? There's nothing you can do for them now." He softened his voice when her eyes began to crinkle. Tears flowed freely down her face. "They're gone."

She began to wail.

"Come on, son," Dan Snr took hold of her left arm. "Let's get her inside."

Her feet dragged as they carried her back to the house. Her head hung low as she sobbed between them. Everyone had gathered in the garage, asking questions, crying, praying, begging for it all to be a bad dream, a hallucination, anything but real. The children were staring at the flames and asking even more questions than their elders. They weren't panicking just yet.

"Get inside," Jack said. "Everybody get inside. Please."

Dan Snr brought Marcy over to Wilma. "Take them back inside, my love.

Watch her carefully. I'm gonna put out the fire."

"Jesus—"

"I'll do that," Jack said. "I'll put out the fire. You need to stay with them, Dad."

"Jackie—"

"Stay with them!" Jack crossed the garage, went around the car to the work bench on the other side. He unhooked the fire extinguisher from its mount on the wall and hurried back through the door onto the driveway. By then, Wilma had herded the kids back up the stairs and clung to Marcy as she brought her in after them. Dan Snr and Cassandra lingered.

"Jack." The flames reflected in her tearful eyes. "Jack, what... what happened?"

"Deb went crazy. I don't know what happened. Get inside, okay? I'll be right there. Dad, you too."

"I'm staying with you, son."

"There's only one extinguisher. There's nothing you can do except get in my way. Take my wife inside."

"Jack—"

Jack kissed his wife. "I love you. Please go back inside. I'll be right there."

76

Deb's Astro blew to pieces. The thunderous sound shook the house. A few of the children screamed. Jack shouted, "Get inside, *now*! It's not safe out here!" Hannah was running out of the group screaming for her dad. Jack grabbed her. "You never listen! Go! *Go*! Back to the house!" Hannah wriggled out of his grip and tried to run around him, but he took hold of her arm and yanked her back harder than intended.

"Dad! Ow! *Daaaaad*!"

"Cassandra!"

Cassandra wrapped an arm around Hannah's waist and carried her kicking and screaming back to the house.

Dan Snr made room for Cassandra and dodged one of Hannah's flying feet as she was carried up the stairs back into the foyer. "We… we need to call an ambulance," he said, more to himself than anyone who could have heard him over Hannah's bawling.

Jack waited until the foyer's door was shut before he dashed across the driveway to the flames. He yanked the pin and sprayed white foam all around the four burning vehicles. He flooded their melting interiors as best he could, wincing and shying away when the heat got too intense. He sprayed the figure that got out of the pickup. He sprayed Deb's remains. He sprayed the truck.

When the extinguisher was empty, the fires were almost completely out. A few orange tongues persisted within the vehicles' black, shriveled husks. Thick clouds of smoke roiled around him, stinging his eyes, consuming the driveway in a black, acrid shroud. Hot surfaces hissed as materials bubbled and liquefied.

Jack coughed, covering his face in the crook of his elbow. He squinted through the smoke at what remained of his relatives.

There wasn't much left of Deb. Her clothing and flesh had all but burned away, and whatever hadn't completely burned clung to her skeleton in charred, shapeless clumps. Even now, a few strands of bubbled skin were stretched taut between her skull and hanging jaw, forming something that could have been a gleeful, silent laugh. Jack stared at her longer than he'd intended, or ever wanted to.

"What the hell did you do?" he rasped. He couldn't tell if it was grief or

78

the smoke that caused tears to pour from his eyes. "What'd you *do*? Jesus, Deb. Jesus…"

He still couldn't figure out who had crawled out of the cab. He bent on one knee, leaning on the empty extinguisher, and peered inside the pickup. He could barely see anything in the heavy smoke billowing out of everything. He could make out a few shapes, a couple of heads and shoulders…

No survivors. For some reason he hoped for a Christmas miracle. Hoped maybe one of them had somehow flown out of the pickup when it was airborne and popped up from behind the trees with a broken leg. Or something. *Something*.

Jack moaned in anguish. In a surge of anger, he hurled the extinguisher across the trail. It landed somewhere in the trees near the pond. He threw his head up and swore at the sky, cursing every deity he could think of for the senselessly cruel direction the night had taken. His voice echoed in the trees and came back to him. It was as if the forest itself was mocking him for his outburst with the same profanities he'd spouted. Something about

79

the echo sounded off. Jack stopped his shouting tirade and listened for the echo, which ended mid-sentence. He heard a branch snap. He stared into the woods behind the pond. Nothing moved in the grey stillness of the wintery scene.

It was cold and empty out here. Jack felt very much alone. He felt utterly useless. He glanced back at the smouldering wreckage and cried. He wiped his tears away, smearing soot across his face. More tears rolled down his cheeks, warm for a moment, then freezing to his face. He went back in the house, locked the garage door and went through the foyer. When he entered the kitchen, he heard cries of anguish and confusion from children and adults alike. Marcy was inconsolable in her chair by the window, flanked by Cassandra and Wilma, who weren't doing much better themselves. The children stood around the table. The younger ones, Harry and Martin, looked confused, scared; while the older ones, Alistair, Brian, and Hannah, understood what had happened, and cried next to their mothers. Alistair was doing his best to suppress his tears, but he was failing miserably. Cassandra noticed

80

Alistair's struggle and pulled him into her bosom in a comforting embrace. He sobbed into her shoulder, trembling. Cassandra looked up at Jack, looking just as hurt and confused as the rest of them.

"Did any of them…?" She couldn't finish her question.

He shook his head 'no' and watched, with growing remorse, as his wife buried her face in their son's hair and cried.

"Did anyone call the cops?"

"I did," Wilma answered from her wailing daughter's side.

"Where's Dad?" Jack asked.

Wilma's voice was tinged with venom. He'd never heard that kind of spite from her before. "Where the hell do you *think*?"

Jack immediately turned and stormed back through the foyer. He threw open the door and slammed it shut behind him. He jumped off the stairs and briskly made for the basement door. He wrenched it open and bounded heavily down the stairs, blinded by tears. He slipped and grabbed hold of the rail to prevent himself from falling. He wiped his eyes, and then continued the rest of the way. Touching cement, he almost *flew* over the work bench. His father was glued to that TV again, his back facing his son, and if he had just sat himself a few inches closer to the work bench, Jack would have yanked him over it by his collar.

"What the fuck is wrong with you?!" Jack hollered.

Dan Snr rotated on his stool, seemingly unperturbed by his son's outburst. "I beg your pardon?"

"My brother, in-laws and nephew are lying dead in that driveway, and the only fucking thing you can think about is your fucking *work*?"

"Yes, Jack. I know how it looks."

"How can you be so fucking *cool* about it? That's your son out there! *My brother*! And his kid! And our in-law! *In-laws*! Don't you care?"

"Of course I care," Dan Snr shot back. Finally, he was showing some emotion through the cracks. To Jack, it seemed like a practiced performance rather than genuine care. "But if I allow myself time to grieve, many more of us will die."

"Fuck you, and fuck your work!" Jack swung his fist at his father's jaw,

82

missed, and swept several stacks of papers and the 'TO WHOM IT MAY CONCERN' envelope off the work table. They crashed to the floor. "Four of us are dead already! I've just about had it with you and your goddamned 'faces in the snow' and your weird fucking cover-up bullshit. They need you upstairs."

"They need me *downstairs*, Jackie, trust me."

"Trust *you*?" Jack seethed.

"You don't understand. We're surrounded! I tried to tell Wilma, I really *tried* to tell her, but she just wouldn't believe me!"

"Believe *what*?"

Dan Snr jumped off his stool and pounded his knuckles against the television screen. He turned around and pointed at it, as if it had all the answers. "Don't you see? They're coming! The cultists are coming! Somehow, they know! Somehow, they've found out about my work. They know I'm on to them. They know, and now they're coming! They got Deb, they turned her, made her kill Junior and Marcus and John; and they'll get the rest of us if we don't find a way to stop them!"

83

"There is no 'them,' and there is no 'we,' between you and me! There's just the kids, my wife, and Mom up there. Grieving, Dad. The cops are on their way. They'll figure it out."

"The cops," Dan Snr echoed, staring at the ceiling fixtures. "The cops... that's it."

"*What* is?!"

"None of you should have come here! If you hadn't, only we would have died. Wilma and I, we're old, we only had a few years left, if that, but you? Junior? Marcy? And your kids? You all had your lifetimes ahead of you."

"Shut up!" Jack lurched around the work table and grabbed Dan Snr by the collar of his shirt. They fell against the TV, nearly knocked it off the desk. "Fuck, you're insane! You're fucking *insane!*" Jack hadn't noticed Dan Snr reaching back and grabbing the revolver. "You insane, paranoid, idiotic son of a bitch! You always prioritized work over us! What the *fuck* is so *fucking important*—"

Dan Snr whipped the revolver's butt across Jack's head. Stunned, Jack let go of his shirt and slipped backwards on a few

84

sheets of paper. Staggering, reaching out to grab something. "Careful. Careful." Dan Snr wrapped his arm around his son's shoulders and led him over the mess to an office chair. He deposited him into the office chair and stood over him. "How're you feeling?"

Jack's eyes rolled upwards, dazed, unfocused. "Dad... did you...?"

"Hit you with the blunt end of a revolver? Yes, Jackie boy, I did. And if you don't keep calm, I'll be forced to do it again. Be right back." Dan Snr returned to his clutter. Jack heard a drawer scrape open and then slam shut, shaking a variety of trinkets on the desk.

"What are you doing, Dad?"

Dan Snr didn't answer. He returned with something silver in his hands, tearing it open loud enough to hurt Jack's ears. "What is that?" Jack asked.

"Nothing." Dan Snr wrapped it around Jack's right arm, securing it to the arm of the chair. He tore off the end and fastened Jack's left arm to the chair. He bent down, duct-taped Jack's ankles together under the seat, his feet resting on the chair's wheeled legs. "Now that you are secure, let me show you what's so important about my wrok. I can share what I know with you. Maybe then you'll understand a little of what's going on, here."

"Why did you tie me to the chair?" Jack's head throbbed painfully. "What the hell is wrong with you? Dad?"

"If you start screaming, I'll close up your mouth, too. I'd rather not do that." Bewildered, Jack watched his father shuffle around the shelves and pull out a slide projector situated on a wheeled cart. He pointed it at the wall by the gun case and turned it on. "I need to make damn sure that you and I are on the same page, son. Tell me—did you see anything weird tonight?"

Images of the fire, the explosion; the shrill, howling screams—Jack started trembling. "You mean... when Deb went fucking insane?"

"Before that. Think before that. Was there anything out of the ordinary? Anything at all?"

Jack thought. He shuddered at the memory of the prankster that ran off into the woods. That's all it was, right? "There

86

was a guy."

"A guy? Describe him."

"Couldn't make out any details about him. Or them. I think there were two of them. Just a couple dumb kids being pranksters."

"What was their 'prank,' Jack? Hurry."

"They were standing outside of the house. The first one was behind the garden, but when I got close to him, he ran off."

"What did you do?"

"I chased him."

"Didja catch him?"

"No. I lost him."

"You're sure?" Dan Snr eyed him carefully.

Jack met his father's eye and, disturbed by his expression, answered slowly, "I'm sure. I couldn't see him, so I went back to the house a-and checked all the doors."

"Why?"

"Made sure they were locked."

"What about the other one?"

"Saw him on the front lawn. He got away, too. He was fast, too, I mean *really* fast."

"You're sure you didn't touch them?"

"No."

Dan Snr's chest heaved as he suppressed his frustration. "No, you're not sure, or no, you didn't touch them?"

"I didn't touch them. Can you untie me now?"

"Not yet."

"Jesus Christ, Dad."

"You told the truth, which is a positive. You remember those surveillance feeds? The ones behind you? I saw the whole thing. I had to know if you would try to lie about it."

"Dad…"

"Quiet. Look at what I have to show you." Dan Snr lifted a remote and pushed a button. The VCR hummed and clicked. The spools whined as they turned. The videotape housed inside of it began to roll, its footage projected across the wall, a static snowstorm morphing into a skinless face wearing heart-shaped sunglasses, the corners of its mouth pinned back in the twisted parody of a grin with diaper pins. The wearer of this face wore a blood-spattered raincoat. He reached behind the camera and the footage jolted and whirled

88

around what looked like a dark basement lined with shelving units. These shelves were stocked full of black clamshell cases with labels on their spines. A mattress could be seen in the far corner. Someone chained to the wall struggled on it. A small girl who couldn't have been older than five or six. She kicked and screamed silently, as the footage had no synchronized sound, only a nauseating low-frequency ambience emitting from it. Another figure in black appeared from the left holding an electric knife over the girl, whose struggles increased in ferocity. The cameraman and his companion descended on the girl.

Jack recoiled in disgust, confusion, and horror. He made a strange gurgling noise and started gagging.

The video suddenly cut to the backyard of a single-floor bungalow with its lights off. A round, above-ground swimming pool bordered by a wooden deck that hugged a third of it had been installed at the back of the house, but now, they were surrounded by holes dug up all around. The footage trembled, as if whoever was filming couldn't keep still. Heads began to rise out of the holes, all of them gazing at the

89

camera. All of them with the same face and long black hair.

Jack shuddered under their piercing glares. He looked down at the floor.

"Don't look away. Look at it. Look at her. Look at *them*."

The scene changed like a before-and-after montage—the heads vanished but the holes remained, and the Morgan house transformed from a well-kept bungalow to a fire-blackened, empty husk with the swimming pool empty and smashed open, and a basement that had swallowed most of the wreckage. Jack felt himself tense when he noticed the outlines of hands protruding from various openings in the charred support beams and warped siding.

A new shot of a little boy no older than seven held his open palm facing down over a flower pot filled with soil. A green stem sprouted from the soil with some kind of time-lapse effect, its buds blooming into a bright-red blood orchid, seemingly birthed under the boy's mental guidance.

The video cut to a big wood grain console TV sitting isolated in the middle of an otherwise austere grey room with dull wallpaper. Something reached through the

90

screen.

Another cut. This time to a crematorium on a hill in a cemetery. Jack could see that the entire building was covered in strange lacerations and deep gashes in its old brick walls. The door had been torn to splinters. Nearby tombstones had been crushed and smashed.

Cut to an underground car park. A woman with short blonde hair was approaching her car from a distance, seemingly unaware of whoever was filming her in that moment. She wore black. She looked very small and vulnerable within the forest of cinderblock pillars, beneath an impenetrable canopy of pipes, light fixtures, and concrete. She reached her car and glanced tentatively around and spotted the camera. She stared at it, tense, the whites of her eyes visible despite the grainy, low-quality film being used to capture her. She was still for several seconds. Then she jolted, startled by a noise Jack couldn't hear. She turned and scrambled out of sight. Dark, humanoid blurs gave chase.

Another cut to an L-shaped roadside motel, filmed from the road. Jack recognized it as the motel on the edge of town by the highway. He'd heard things about arsonists and drug addicts from the news. Now, he was seeing it before the fire. Strange shapes shuffled within the shadows in its parking lot. The lights in the breakfast nook and connected lobby were bright through wall-to-ceiling windows despite the shades being half-drawn. The neon sign above the parking lot entrance flickered. There were no vacancies, but more figures seemed to flood in from the blackness of the ditch.

Another cut. The camera panned over harsh white light and grimy tiles. It was filthy, revolting. It was such a mess that he couldn't quite tell what was going on in it, but the grimy textures shone grotesquely in strobe-like blurs. Tiles. He could see some tiles. Some had been torn out. Some were smeared with blood and feces. A pair of tiny legs splayed out in a white porcelain sink flashed by. The bathtub beside it was stained black and yellow, layered in gleaming liquids and solids covered in pustules and dark splotches. The camera peered down into the toilet, which was clogged with much of the same, only it had a small, smooth, round, yellow cranium half-submerged in it. The sight nauseated Jack. The strobing effect, the poor video quality, the swooping camera angles, and the imagery of brutal death amidst human filth and decay gave him cold sweats and a violently roiling stomach.

Jack felt a horrible buzzing sound as his very nerves reacted to what he was seeing. Tears streamed down his cheeks. The persistent white noise filled his ears and seemed to get louder, more high-pitched. He could feel it buzzing in his skull like bees trying to escape a burning nest. Behind that persistent frequency, Jack could make out a few words. Something in the sound was whispering to him, mostly drowned out by dense white noise, which deepened into an overpowering ambience that vibrated in his bones.

The camera swooped through a doorway into a dark room lit only by a television set, from which protruded a human head. The screen was intact, yet the head was attached to a neck that seemed to extend into the TV, as if someone had managed to pass through the screen. It was a boy's head. The boy had curly dark hair.

93

The cameraman approached the boy, whose eyes widened with unbridled fear at the camera's POV. A butcher knife blurred across the frame and the boy's head dropped from the screen to the floor. The television set bled profusely from the bottom of the frame, the static snow turning pink.

"Jesus, no," Jack gasped, watering eyes bulging, unblinking.

The head rolled onto its stump and sprouted ten spindly little spider legs from beneath his jawline.

"What—"

The head tried to crawl away, only for a silent flash of harsh light to reduce the creature into flying chunks of flesh and bone. The camera suddenly panned up to a tall, frail-looking woman framed in a doorway, backlit by a bulb in the kitchen behind her. Her face was distended in screaming terror, her eyes piercing the dark shadows that masked her front. Arms at her sides, elbows inwards, fingers unnaturally long and curled, hands swinging back and forth as she screamed. Some of the boy's head splashed on her, glistening wetly as they reflected the TV screen's strobe-like

94

patterns.

"No!" Jack screamed. "No! Don't make me look at that!" Tears poured down his face. Jack threw his head back and sucked in air to howl when his father's hand stifled his cries by burrowing straight down his throat. He choked on his father's grimy fingers wriggling around, spasmodic in the chair.

Dan Snr cut his hand on Jack's teeth. He ripped his hand out and slapped his other palm over his son's mouth. He stooped down, wrapped his arm around his neck as Jack continued his struggle. "Stop screaming! I told you what would happen if you fucking screamed!" He struck Jack's head in the same place as before. Jack's screams dissolved into terrible moans. Dan Snr grabbed the duct tape, slapped it over Jack's mouth, and looped it around Jack's head four times before cutting it.

Jack's cries were muffled by the tape pressing into every side of his head.

"Pay attention," Dan Snr said. "This is important stuff."

The door at the top of the stairs opened. Cassandra called down, "Jack? Dad?"

Jack screamed through the duct tape as loud as he could before Dan Snr swatted him across his head.

"Jack?" Cassandra cried out.

Jack tore his left hand free from the arm of the chair and swiped his father's gun out of his hand. The revolver clattered under one of the shelving units.

"Stupid bastard!" Dan Snr cursed him. Dan Snr fell on his knees and desperately pawed the bottom tier of the shelf, trying to squeeze his fingers under it. "Damn!"

Jack's fingers on his freed hand dug under the tape stuck to his cheek and yanked hard enough to painfully uproot the stubble he'd neglected to shave that morning. He bit on the section over his mouth as best he could as he yanked, feeling his facial hair peel away with it.

Dan Snr swore in frustration and shoved the entire shelving unit against the other shelves lined up behind it. A loud crash filled the basement, assaulting everyone's ears.

"What's going on down there?" Cassandra sounded frightened. She started down the stairs. Jack saw her right foot

96

appear on the step just below ceiling level and grimaced. He ripped the tape around his head in two and tore it away from his face. It stuck to the back of his head. "Cassandra, get back upstairs!"

Cassandra's feet paused on the staircase.

Dan Snr came back with the revolver. "Stop this, Jack! I'm not going to hurt any of you." He had a videotape in his hands. A strange, black fluid dripped from it onto his hand and slithered around his thumb and down his arm. "Look at this. *Look* at it, you damned, stubborn little prick!"

Jack pulled his right hand through his bonds and drove his fist into his father's left knee. Dan Snr groaned and collapsed on all fours in front of his son. Jack clenched his fists together in a ball, raised it over his head, and brought it down between Dan Snr's shoulder blades. Dan Snr gasped heavily as he thudded against the concrete floor.

Cassandra rushed down the stairs and gasped in horror at the sight of Dan Snr on the floor. When she saw Jack still tied to the chair, the horror made way for frightened confusion, and the collage of horrible images projected onto the far wall confused her further. "Jesus—Jack, what happened? What's going on?"

"Dad went crazy. Tied me to this chair." Jack pressed his hand against his face and was shocked by the bright red staining his palm. "Kept... kept hitting me."

"Oh, my God." Cassandra's wide eyes surveyed the chaos of the basement. "Oh, my God."

"Help me. My legs're still tied." Jack heard his father groan on the floor. "Hurry."

Cassandra rushed toward him, stumbled over Dan Snr's slow, writhing form.

"Careful," Jack told her.

She paused as the images on the wall drew her attention. Her eyes widened at the sight of something crawling across a cement floor.

"Don't look at it. Cass, untie me."

"Watch him." Cassandra started undoing the wrinkled tape wrapped tightly around her husband's ankles.

"I'm watching him. Hurry."

"He tied it tight."

98

"Screw it. Get the gun."

"The *what*?"

"The *gun*, Cass, get the gun before he comes to!"

Cassandra scrambled away from the chair and wrenched the revolver out of Dan Snr's grasp.

"Give it to me." She obeyed. "Now my feet, please, baby. Hurry." He held the gun in his father's rough direction, pointing it above the old man and keeping his finger off the trigger. He didn't want to accidentally shoot him. He was still his father, despite his violent, delirious outburst. Jack was a lot more hurt and confused by it than he was angry.

Cassandra kept sneaking glances at Dan Snr as he groaned and rolled on his back, his arms rigid. Finally, she freed Jack's ankles from the chair and helped him on his feet. His legs wobbled; the room was running laps around him. "I gotcha." Cassandra draped his arm over her shoulders and led him toward the stairs.

"Wait," he said. Using the back of the chair to steady himself, he stumbled to the VCR, fumbled with it until the images stopped flickering on the wall, and tucked it under his arm.

"The children," Dan Snr moaned. "They're after the children!"

Jack took steady hold of the staircase railing. "Get the shotgun, honey."

Cassandra stared at him, wide-eyed. Then she nodded, showing she understood, and ran past Dan Snr to the gun case around the corner. She grabbed the shotgun.

"The shells," Jack said, unaware that she was already in the process of scooping up as much ammo as she could carry. "Get the shells."

"Got 'em." Cassandra ran up beside him, cradling the shotgun and boxes of ammunition for both guns, spilling shells on the floor. Together they went up the stairs, ignoring Dan Snr's raving about the children's safety behind them.

Jack slammed the door shut. The garage's ceiling rafters rattled from the impact. When the couple returned to the foyer, he locked the door to the garage behind them.

100

Friday, December 15th, 2000 - Part V

Cassandra spilled everything across the kitchen counter. Shells clattered on linoleum flooring. Alistair was standing by the counter with a glass of tap water. When he saw the guns and shells, he said, "Cool!"

An irate Jack snarled, "*Get* back in the living room!"

Sullen, Alistair did as he was told.

"That was uncalled for, Jack." Wilma was dabbing the bloody welts on Jack's head with a damp cloth, parting mats of his hair in the process.

Jack replied, "He's old enough to know better."

"He's *eight*," Wilma retorted. "He's not hurting anyone." As she continued to dab at Jack's wound, she shook her head in disbelief, blinking tears away as best she could. "He would never," she said. "I can't believe he hit you."

Jack winced every time his mother pressed the cloth on his welts. He grumbled, "Didn't think he would, either, but I guess the old man's full of surprises

101

these days. He hasn't walloped me like that since I was twelve."

"It was never like this," Wilma said. "Dan never made you bleed."

"It's that damned research." Cassandra dropped the shotgun on the table loudly, sending a few shells rolling over the edge. The sound startled Marcy, causing her to spill some wine all over her arm. Marcy seemed entranced by the wine that soaked her arm. Strangely, she said nothing about the stain it was going to leave on her clothes. Cassandra apologized to her and stooped down to pick up the fallen shelves.

"Is he still locked downstairs?" Wilma wet the rag under hot water from the faucet, wrung out the excessive water, and pressed it against Jack's welts again. "Hold that there."

Jack raised his right hand to keep it in place, sighing heavily. "We should go home."

"We can't just leave..." Marcy's voice trailed away. Her eyes, glassy from the alcohol she was consuming or grief or a mixture of both; fell to her glass.

"Is he still locked down there?" Wilma asked again.

"Yeah," Jack answered her. He strained forward on his chair, scowling at the table. "Well, not so much locked down there, but he's locked *out* of here. Can't get the rest of us. The old son of a bitch's gone crazy, looking at all that shit from the police station. This." He raised the videotape for all of them to see. "Hopefully that'll bring him back to his senses."

"What's on it?" Wilma asked.

"You don't wanna know. Old fuck made me watch some of it."

"Don't call him that. He's still your father," Wilma hissed. "He still deserves your respect."

"No," Jack snapped back, pointing at his head. "Not if he does *this*, Mom! Fuck that guy. The stuff on this tape is some of the vilest shit I've ever seen. Nobody should've been looking through it as long as he has."

Marcy extended her arm. "Lemme see that."

Cassandra took it out of Jack's hand and placed it in Marcy's.

"Don't watch it," Jack said. "Seriously."

"I'm just looking at it." Marcy

103

studied every side of it and grimaced in disgust. "Why's it wet?"

"You have wine all over you."

Marcy looked at her hands and confirmed it. "Yeah, that must be it." She read the white label aloud, "'Sleepwatchers #7'? 'Sleepwatchers'. Isn't that a Stephen King movie?" She scoffed and placed it on the table. As she wiped her hands dry with a tissue, she said, "Looks like somebody taped it off the TV and made a bunch of copies."

Wilma took a seat next to Marcy. She was breathing heavily, her shoulders shuddering uncontrollably as she suppressed her tears.

Cassandra cupped her husband's face in her hands in a consoling gesture. "Jack…"

"What?"

She planted a kiss on his forehead. "Everything will be okay."

"No," he said, holding her closely, tightly. "Not until I know what the hell's going on. He thinks he knows what's happening to us. Those people hanging around the house. Deb's psychotic… whatever that was… he thinks it's all

104

connected."

"With what?"

"The weird shit that's been happening in this township over the past few years. Horrible shit." Jack shuddered as the images crept into his mind again.

"The projector," Cassandra said, "I saw it."

Wilma turned in her chair. She couldn't stop her tears anymore. They rolled down her wrinkled, weathered face. To see someone as gentle as her breaking down felt like a knife had been jammed into Jack's heart. "What did he show you?"

"I don't want to say, Mom. It was horrific. It was... I can't even really put it into words."

"Try."

Jack sat there, pressing his face against his wife's bosom, staring blankly at the oven and the refrigerator embedded among the polished wood cabinets and drawers.

"What did you see, Jack?" Wilma pressed.

Jack's arms tightened around his wife. He shivered as Cassandra ran her fingers through his hair behind the damp

105

cloth in an effort to calm him. It didn't help. He heard the children sobbing in the next room and raised his head, turned it, forcing Cassandra to move her arm out of his field of vision. "The kids," he said.

"The kids?" Wilma asked. "He showed you the kids?"

"No. They came all this way to... to see you and Dad. Cops should be here soon, right? We'll take them home once the cops take care of things here."

Cartoon shenanigans on the screen failed to get laughs from any of them.

Marcy left her spot at the table and put great effort into comforting Brian and Hannah, assuring them that everything would be fine, they'd be home soon.

Cassandra tended to her own children while Jack watched from the island counter in the kitchen, still holding the cloth against his aching head.

Eventually, Jack's gaze wandered away from his wife and children to the window looking out into the backyard. Snow began to fall in fuzzy white drifts across the trees, tumbling onto the back deck. His father's pleas entered his mind, shrill and desperate, as he held up that

106

videotape which seemed to secrete black fluid. He wondered about it; what got on it—or in it—to make it leak that kind of oily substance? Maybe Dan Snr had dropped the tape in something and mistook it for something else?

"Look at it, you damned, stubborn prick!" he'd screamed, as if it held all the proof he needed to convince Jack that he wasn't crazy.

Maybe it did.

Jack decided he had to know. He stepped off the chair and picked up the shotgun, loaded it with a few shells, and shoved another handful of them in his pocket.

Alarmed by this, Marcy, Cassandra, and Wilma all crowded around him at once, demanding an explanation, asking him what was wrong with him.

"What's got into you?" Wilma was nearly shouting. "That's your *father* down there!"

"It's just for my protection," Jack explained, though he knew he wasn't about to convince any of them that that was all the shotgun was for. "It's a deterrent. I'm not gonna shoot my father."

Marcy scoffed with loud indignation. "Could've fooled me."

"Jack." Cassandra tried to pry the shotgun out of his hands. "Jack, why?"

"Stop it." He jerked the gun away from them, making sure his finger was off the trigger and the barrel was pointed at the window in case of accidental discharge. No one else would die tonight if he had anything to say about it. "I need answers. I want to know what's so damn important that he'd go the extra mile to try and show me."

"I'm coming with you," Cassandra said as she reached for the revolver she'd set on the table next to the box of shells and some strawberry pastries.

"No. All of you need to stay up here with the kids. Keep a lookout for those weirdos. Dad said they're coming back."

"And you believe him?"

"I don't know. All I know is that he seems to be the only one here who has any idea what's going on. Crazy or not…" Jack shrugged, giving everyone a doubtful look.

Cassandra's voice rose agitatedly. "You wanna talk deterrence? Two people are better than one. Either I'm coming with

108

you, or you're staying up here. Which is it?"

Jack's eyes pleaded silently with his mother and sister for help, but the vacant looks on their faces told him they wouldn't try to stop his wife. She'd made her decision and they were more than content with staying upstairs with the children. "Fine," he said, admitting defeat. "I guess you're right."

Cassandra wasn't the type to stand around and boast every time she got her way. She grabbed the revolver and immediately started into the foyer. Jack trailed behind her. They slipped into their boots together before they entered the cold dampness of the garage. The sound of the door shutting behind them seemed to echo in the sanded rafters.

Cassandra shuddered. "It's cold in here."

"Dad keeps the basement warm." Jack carefully opened the door to the basement and peered down the stairs. It was silent down there, though he could hear the high-pitched frequency being emitted from his father's television on his desk. "Dad?" he called, but there was no answer.

"Dad?"

Silence.

Jack exhaled through his nose, working up the courage to take the first step down those stairs. "Come on," he whispered to his wife, and gripped the shotgun with both hands as he descended the steps with stooped back and bent knees. "I'm coming down, Dad." He drummed his fingertips against the shotgun's cold steel. "Don't try anything stupid." The next board groaned under his foot. "I'm armed." Another step crackled slightly. "I'll shoot you if you leave me with no other choice. You hear me?"

He stopped when the room came into view. It was as if the struggle had never happened; the shelves were all upright and once again filled with tapes and documents and books. The duct tape had been removed from the office chair, which was tucked under the desk. The work table stood rigidly under towers of documents, boxes, papers, and photographs. Behind the desk, Jack saw a face. Starkly pale and framed between bangs of short blonde hair, her eyes bulging further out of her sockets than Jack thought was possible for a human

110

being. There was pitch blackness behind her. The picture's distortion caused her head to wobble into strange, wiggling shapes that danced across the television screen around her eyes. Her stare burned through the static like a pair of laser dots, seemingly unaffected by the warped quality of the image. Jack couldn't look away from those eyes. There was something about her...

Cassandra shouted in surprise, snapping Jack out of his trance, as Dan Snr leaped up from behind the desk and hurled something at them. A black object. Jack dodged it and heard it whistle by his face, watched it smash wetly into the concrete wall. Its arteries ruptured from within its plastic case, splashing black goo. A spool of film tumbled out of the videotape as its chunky fragments hit the floor. Jack watched the reels bounce out from their housing and roll back toward the desk, unspooling little black entrails of film behind them.

Jack lurched in disgust and horror at the pulsating organs spewing black and red puss out of the shattered cassette. Heart, kidney, stomach, intestines all seemed to

111

have been crammed into the videocassette at one point, now burst free from their plastic confinement. Beneath the fluorescent ceiling light tubes, the cassette's steaming innards gleamed with a sickly sheen. The intestines slithered out from the bubbling mass, rising up like curious snakes flicking their forked tongues in the air. Jack couldn't look away from the thing. Every instinct told him to shoot it and run. He remained petrified. He couldn't even hear Cassandra screaming at the sight.

Dan Snr smashed it with a spade, startling the couple further. He brought it up and slammed the spade down on the thing in the videotape mercilessly, up, down, up, down—until the videocassette carapace had been completely destroyed, and the organs had all been reduced to mush.

Dan Snr breathed heavily. He stood his shovel upright and leaned on the handle. He asked the stunned couple with noticeable coolness, "Do you believe me now?"

"What…" Jack could barely form the words. "What was *that*?"

"*That* was what I was talking about."

112

The revolver rattled in Cassandra's shaking hand. She had sense enough to keep her finger on the trigger guard and the business end pointed at the floor. "You're sick. Were those deer guts? Did you shove deer guts inside of a videotape to prove some kind of point?"

Jack jumped quickly to his father's defence. "No. Those organs were hot. They were moving. It was *alive*. Whatever it is, it isn't a deer."

Dan Snr watched them carefully as the two of them bent down to take a closer look. "Not too close," Jack instructed his wife.

"It's safe," Dan Snr assured them. "She's dead."

"'She'?" Jack gaped at his father. "You gave it a gender? What, did you give it a name, too?"

"It's a little hard to explain…"

They inspected the corpse of the videotape abomination for a few seconds longer. Jack prodded it curiously with the shotgun.

"D-don't poke it." Cassandra felt a wave of nausea and shuddered, turning away with her hand over her mouth. Dan

Snr quickly pulled out the office chair and wheeled it over to her.

"Sit. Sit. It's okay." After gently coaxing Cassandra to sit down, Dan Snr turned to face his son.

Jack tore his eyes away from the smashed videocassette and its unnaturally gory state, tasting bile, fighting the urge to vomit. He clamped his eyes shut and steadied his breathing, doing his best to think about Christmas cookies, flowers, caramel popcorn, anything that kept his food down. After he'd composed himself, he said to his father: "I'm listening."

114

Friday, December 15th, 2000 - Part VI

From storage, Dan Snr took out a large, old fish tank, from a time in Jack's childhood when they kept multiple goldfish as pets; and placed it on the desk. He scraped the pile of crushed organs and cassette fragments with the spade and dropped them into the box. Then he locked the box shut and left it out in the open. He switched off the TV set on the work bench.

Cassandra wearily avoided looking at the glistening mass of wet, malformed flesh her father-in-law had contained.

The first thing Dan Snr went for in his collection of evidence was the massive envelope that had caught Jack's eye earlier. He handed it to Jack, and Jack read its title tentatively, "'To Whom It May Concern'? Why're you giving me this?"

"I saw you eyeballing it."

"So what?"

"Read it."

"Why?"

Dan Snr exhaled impatiently through his nostrils. "It's Cameron Morgan's own personal diary. He started writing it sometime after it all started for him."

"When *what* started?"

His father gave him a stern look. "Something that seems to resemble our own problem. Except... he found a way to live with it for a few long years."

Jack took the envelope and laid it flat on the desk, opened it, and began to read through its opening paragraphs aloud, setting each finished page face down in a separate stack:

"'Wednesday, November 12th, 1997... Maureen has been acting strangely these past few weeks, and it's gotten to the point where she's hitting the kids over small things, like when Michael wet the bed yesterday. She never used to lay a hand on those kids. Now, it seems like anything will set her off. I'm going to attempt a romantic getaway for just the two of us in a couple of days, and see if that helps things at all. Something's bothering her,

116

but I can't figure it out and she refuses to tell me. She keeps insisting that she's okay. But I know she isn't.

"'Thursday, November 13th, 1997… Michael wet himself at school today. It wasn't a big deal. We've been supplying him with a spare pair of pants just in case. But Maureen was infuriated. I'd never seen her so angry before. She started hitting him when he told us. I tried to stop her, but she was unusually strong and strangely heavy for a 140-pound woman. Michael locked himself in the bathroom, and Maureen, in white-hot pursuit, tried to break down the bathroom door, screaming insults and death threats. She was pure fire and brimstone.

"'By the time it was all over, she'd punched several holes in the hallway's walls, even left claw marks in some of

117

the doors. The kids are terrified. I'm not too far from feeling the same way. Whoever Maureen has become, she's not the woman I married. There's something wrong with her. The way she sits still for hours, staring into space. Her eyes never move, except when one of the kids walks by her, and then her eyes follow them with this predatory gaze that, honestly, terrifies me. I feel her violent thoughts toward our children through that hateful, wide-eyed gaze she's been practicing. I don't know what the hell her problem is, but I'm going to try to reason with her, somehow. If that doesn't work, I'll have to turn her in to the boys at the station.

"'Friday, November 14th, 1997... It got worse. I had to lock Maureen out of the house tonight. She screamed and cried and pleaded for me to let

118

her back in. I sat in the kitchen and listened to her howling echo in the trees until morning. Surprisingly, none of our neighbours called the police to file a noise complaint. I found that strange, as she was louder than any wolf or coyote that could have come from around here. She sounded like she was being murdered, so I was often compelled to look through the windows to check on her. She always seemed to notice me looking out at her, no matter where she was, no matter how well hidden I was in the house with the lights off—her howling would stop, and I could feel her eyes watching me from the dark woods that surrounded us. It was just a feeling at first, but I knew for sure once I stepped out of sight, because the howling would continue until I looked out again.

"'She was tormenting me. Whatever her intention,

119

whatever she was becoming, she had some sort of heightened awareness and aggression towards me, more so towards the kids. Every time I hid myself in the darkness, she would laugh. No matter where I went in the house, her laughter followed me around. I couldn't escape her.

"'By morning, she was fine. Or… she pretended to be fine. It was hard to tell. She seemed so genuinely confused… I scheduled a doctor's appointment for a checkup, followed by a mental health examination. She went to both without any fuss, though she seemed insulted by the implication that she needed them. I wondered if she really somehow forgot about her behaviour, how it would become increasingly erratic as the evenings wore on, to the point of psychopathy by around ten or eleven at night. She

120

would be completely unhinged until about five in the morning. I entertained the idea that it had something to do with her sleeping, or dream states. Hell, maybe it had something to do with the lunar cycle. I couldn't pinpoint it. I wasn't an expert on any of that stuff.

"'I was so hesitant to turn her in. I still am. She's the mother of my children. I've resorted to keeping them away from her, although at this point it doesn't take much to convince them to stay away from her. They're afraid of her now. They want nothing to do with her.'"

Jack flipped through a couple pages, glimpsing minor details on each page as it passed by his line of sight. Some were full of mundanities and ramblings about an increasingly unhinged wife as written by a distraught husband who himself didn't seem much saner than his subject. He read a brief passage about buying padlocks for

121

the children's bedroom doors for their own safety. He paused every once in a while when a word or a phrase caught his eye, and after reading the passages surrounding those words or phrases, he would continue turning the pages until he found one passage that sent shivers through him. He cleared his throat and read it aloud:

> ""...I found her squatting at the foot of the deck stairs along the side of the house. His fur was matted to her face and encrusted in blood that hadn't yet dried or frozen stiff in the winter cold. There was so much of it. The snow was all red and melting under a thinning cloud of steam. She'd torn him apart with her bare hands. She'd eaten Wilbur.'"

"Jack," Cassandra said. "I don't want to hear any more of that."

Jack took a moment to breathe in an attempt to steady himself. He made another turn of the page. After skimming its long, grisly description of the writer's mutilated

122

dog and his own personal conflicts about it, Jack asked his father, "You think this has anything to do with what's going on?"

"I don't *think* it has anything to do with what's going on," Dan Snr replied, "I *know* it does."

"But how? This guy's talking about, about..." Jack stalled, trying to come to terms with it, "some kind of possession?"

"More or less."

"Nobody here's possessed," Jack went on. "We're just the victims of a very annoying prank and a... a very unfortunate circumstance." He froze, then, remembering Deb dancing in the flames that engulfed her as her shrieking laughter filled the air. He shivered and blinked several times to keep the tears at bay. He couldn't believe they were gone, so suddenly, and in such an unforeseen way.

"Deb," Dan Snr whispered, as if he'd read his son's mind. "Deb was acting strangely, wasn't she? Before..."

"Not really. Not until then."

Cassandra spoke up: "Yes. Yes, actually. She wasn't acting like herself. Don't you remember, Jack? When she stood outside without a coat, barefoot in the snow?"

"Yeah, but—"

"No ifs, ands, or buts about it." Cassandra stood, somewhat shakily, from her chair. Her voice was stronger now. "She was acting strange all evening."

"Their influence is already strong. They've got us surrounded." Before anyone could ask who, Dan Snr threw a wrinkled pamphlet at Jack, who caught it and read the title aloud.

"'Holy Ascension Resort'?"

"Disciples of some obscure order. The girl was a member, once."

"What girl?"

"The *girl*, Jack. The one you saw on the TV. Don't act like you didn't see her when you came down the stairs. The girl in the videotape. I just threw her organs at you."

Jack regarded his father with a disturbed look.

"Isn't it crazy?" Dan Snr started pacing around his desk, flipping papers and knocking over a pile of additional 'Sleepwatchers' tapes, all numbered. "Isn't it? Isn't it *crazy*? Some kid rummages through his parents' things and gets it in his

124

head to rape people with it. It's spread like a virus, now. We're all in danger of being infected. That's what they want to stop. They want to bury us with it. I won't let that happen. I won't. You see, we're the gatekeepers. You know what that means?" Before Jack or Deb could answer, Dan Snr went on: "We have them by the balls, kids, we got leverage. They're not gonna storm the house outright because they're afraid we've already opened the gate, but they're not gonna leave, either, because they're even more afraid of us opening it."

Jack took a moment to try to process what he was hearing. "Opening… what?"

"The *gate*, boy, the *gate*! We have the means of releasing it out into our world. Other houses got a tape. They got the keys to unlocking it. No, not the keys, not the keys… the *door*. They got the door. Most of them never really had a chance to open it, I think.

Whether Cameron Morgan received a tape or not—whether he *watched* a tape or not, is irrelevant. He never opened the door. Or at least, if he did, he just didn't see its connection with his circumstances. There's no way to really know. Everything

125

that belonged to Cameron Morgan died in flames. Everything but that manifesto. You saw the videotape. That's one videotape the boys at the station recovered from the Anderson house. Most of them were blank. Probably wiped by a magnet. The Anderson kids were both dead in the basement—one of them had suffered repeated, relentless sexual abuse. You saw it. Their parents are still missing to this day, despite reports of Donna Anderson being seen all around town. That face you saw in the TV? It was her. I think she found a way to the other side. I think she's trapped. I think they want her to stay that way. I think that's why they're here. That's why they're after us, to stop us, to burn the rest of the tapes, to keep us from opening the gate and letting her through."

Something tapped the glass. Cassandra yelped and skirted away from the glass box in terror. Jack saw the way she raised the gun and thought for a moment that she was really going to shoot it, but she didn't. Instead, she exclaimed, "Jesus! What *is* all of this? I can't listen to it anymore. It's like it's still alive!"

Jack and Dan Snr approached the

126

desk and peered through the box's glass walls, noticing that the glass would fog up and then clear slightly, only to fog up again, as if the box contained a living, breathing creature.

The organs were intact once more. The videotape's black plastic jutted out of its greasy, purple flesh, like shrapnel in a grenade survivor. The pulpy amalgamation of human organs swathed in a translucent layer of light peach-coloured skin was *breathing*.

"Incredible," Dan Snr gasped.

Jack staggered away from it, shuddering violently. "We have to kill it. How do we kill it? I thought the shovel was all we needed..."

"That's what I assumed," Dan Snr concurred as he leaned over the box. "But apparently she's a bit more durable than that, aren't you, Mrs. Anderson?"

Cassandra blurted, "Don't talk to *it* like it's a human being."

"This 'gateway' thing that you were just talking about," Jack began slowly, "you know, provided I'm gonna actually entertain the plausibility of whatever you just said—if that's her way of getting

127

through to our world from wherever the hell it is she's trapped in…" Jack pointed at the box. "Isn't that her physical manifestation?"

"Yes."

Jack was incredulous. "So you already let her through?"

"Sort of. I think so."

"Are you insane?"

"No. It's a deterrent. They're afraid of her. So long as we keep her reasonably contained—"

"Screw this." Jack jacked a round into the chamber and aimed his shotgun at the box. "I'm blasting her."

"No!" Dan Snr leaped between them.

Jack lifted his finger off the trigger. A surge of anger caused him to bark, "Are you crazy? Get out of the goddamn way!"

"If you shoot her, you forfeit the lives of everyone here."

"I *don't* shoot her, our lives are forfeit anyway, but it'll be *your* fault."

"What if we can contain her?"

"Contain her? She grew out of a *videotape*, Dad. She even regenerated like in those weird little comic books my sons read after you smashed her into paste. I

128

don't think something like that can be held in a glass box. Don't make me shoot through you."

"You wouldn't dare." Dan Snr stood his ground. Jack could see it in the old man's eyes. He wasn't about to move. Jack faltered slightly. Dan Snr could see the hesitation clear as a polished mirror. "Go ahead, son. Go ahead and do it."

Cassandra stepped warily next to them without getting within dangerous range of her husband's shotgun muzzle. "Stop it. Jack. Jack! This is ridiculous. Dad might be right."

"I don't like it." Jack didn't lower the shotgun. "Cass, pull him out of the way."

"Don't think I won't slug you just because you're a woman," Dan Snr said, his eyes wide with warning toward her. "I like you, Cassandra. Let's not change that."

"Dad, if you touch my wife, you might find me pulling the trigger with a lot less hesitation than I'm showing now."

"So do it. Do it and kill yourselves while you're at it. You may as well. She's our only hope out of here. What part of that can't you see?"

"We have zero reason to believe

129

Donna Anderson—if that's even what that thing is—will help us in any way, shape, or form. That thing isn't natural. It's alien, or something."

"She's not an alien. That would be preposterous."

"Oh, *that's* preposterous? That's where we draw the line here?"

"She's *evolved*."

"Fuck 'evolved'. You've been down here away from the sun too long. And why the hell would a cult who's all about 'evolving' want to stop the very thing they're striving to achieve, anyway? That doesn't make any goddamn sense."

"I don't have all the answers, son. I just have what I've seen."

"No. You just have hypotheses. You put everyone in this house at risk if you're wrong."

"And if I'm right, I save the rest of us."

"*If* you're right. I'm not willing to take that risk. We already lost Deb, Dan, John, and Marcus. You wanna lose anyone else here tonight?"

"Do *you*?" Before Jack could come up with a retort, Dan Snr gestured irritably

130

toward the bank of televisions lining the far wall. "Look at the feed. *Look* at it. You too, Cassandra, look into those trees. Look at them all lying in wait." He went over to the TVs himself and drew a wide circle with his arms like a salesman presenting a brand-new car.

The couple drew cautiously toward the screens, making sure to stay out of Dan Snr's reach, and scanned the static shots of the surrounding yards as well as the blackened wreckage in the driveway. The naked trees and white snow provided little camouflage for the prowlers squatting behind the trees from all around them. A peeking head here, a leg there, a shoulder; a few of them were lying flat in the snow, black shadows laid out to their full length, faces down, hoods drawn over abnormally large heads. A few of them had strange light emanating from under their hoods. None of them appeared to be armed, from what little they could see on the cameras.

Cassandra moaned hopelessly, "We really *are* surrounded... oh, God. Oh, *God...!*"

Dan Snr said, "Earlier, I spoke with Donna about them. I was watching them approach the house. They ran away when you chased them, Jack."

"Wait, hold on... you knew I chased them away? Why question me, then?"

"Because I didn't know how much you knew. I needed to know if you knew anything about them."

"This is a first for me," Jack said, his voice dripping with venom. "Sorry to say."

Ignoring his son's last comment, Dan Snr went on: "Connie and Sam packed up and left two weeks ago when they spotted someone trying to sneak across their backyard. All in black like these guys. I read it in the paper. A week later, Chief Harlan brought me all these boxes. There'd been more sightings. Some... intrusions. No fatalities, but a few close calls. With one exception: an entire family is dead. None of this has been in the paper—"

"Why? How?"

"I don't know. It's being suppressed. Probably getting harder for them to suppress it, too, since the incidents have been getting out of hand lately.

"They employ the same method every time, but the outcomes appear to be random. Sometimes the victims come out

132

of it scared, but unscathed. Other times…
well. If they're seen, they usually retreat
back to their hiding place and then try again
from a different spot. It's a game to them.
Psychological warfare. But unlike
everyone else who's found themselves in
our current situation, *we* have the upper
hand."

"How?" Jack gulped. Doubt
remained on his face, but it was beginning
to crumble, exposing fear that was
becoming harder for him to conceal. "That
thing you're growing on the table?"

"As soon as I pulled her through, they
stopped. It's like they could *sense* her
passage from wherever she came from.
Stalemate."

"We have to go," Jack said.

"Go? Go *where*?"

"Anywhere but here."

"How? We can't all fit into Wilma's
car."

"One of us takes the kids outta here.
You and I are staying here. That just leaves
Mom, Cass, or Marcy with the
responsibility to keep their foot on the gas
till they're in Orillia or hell, Oshawa or
Branton. Anywhere but here."

133

Cassandra looked at her husband, but said nothing.

Dan Snr replied, "You want Cass to take them, don't you? Wilma's old, and Marcy doesn't have a husband, just two kids you could fit in there. Cassandra's more than competent. She could take care of them all, at least for a time. Plus, Marcy's damaged goods now, with her husband burning to death before her eyes. Right?" Dan Snr's eyes were boring into him, uncomfortably assured in their silent implications. There was a five-foot gap between them, but somehow it felt like Dan Snr was right in his face, glaring directly into his ulterior motives. "That's what you were thinking, wasn't it?"

"I didn't say that."

Dan Snr took a measured step forward. "But you were *thinking* it."

"You keep back."

Dan Snr didn't take another step. "Of course you would want your wife to get out of this."

"With the kids out, we'll have more flexibility if it came to a full assault on all sides. I don't care if you think this mutant thing is gonna keep them from coming in

134

here; sooner or later they're gonna say 'fuck it' and rush the house. And when that happens, it'll be impossible to protect the kids *and* ourselves. With the kids out of the equation, we'll stand a better chance. Marcy's been drinking all night. And yeah, as much as I hate saying it, Mom's old. She probably wouldn't want to leave here, anyway. I'm staying behind, too. Cass is our best and only logical getaway driver."

"And if they rush the car?"

"You have cameras. We'll know if they try to cut us off."

"They might have guns."

"*We* have guns."

Dan Snr scoffed. "Ridiculous. Utterly ridiculous."

Cassandra, at a loss, asked sardonically, "Why don't we talk to the others and draw straws, huh? We'll let democracy settle this."

"Fuck democracy," Dan Snr snapped at her. "This ain't the time to be making jokes. Time's the only thing we don't have and we've wasted plenty of it down here with this debate. We're already out of it, I think. Our best bet is to fortify the house. Don't even give them a chance to get in or take pot shots at the kids or your wife."

"I'll floor it," Cassandra said.

"Please," Dan Snr spat mockingly, cocking his head slightly with a derisive gleam in his eyes. "You're *floor* it in minus-thirty winter weather on frozen gravel? Good luck. You're more likely to hit a tree than drive out of here with all of you in one piece. And if that were the case, who's to say they won't rush the wreck, pick off what's left? You'll be defenseless, even *if* we have guns." Dan Snr's eyes flicked back to his son, who was once again leveling the shotgun muzzle with the glass case. Instantly, a switch had been flipped— Dan Snr closed the gap between them. "Jack, put that fucking gun down or so help me God I'll—"

He never got to finish his sentence, because Jack had thrown the butt stock of his shotgun into his father's face, hard enough to send him sprawling over the front half of the desk, spilling papers, videotapes; and nearly shoving the glass box onto the floor. "I warned you, old man. Stay out of my way!"

"Jack!" Cassandra shouted, reaching to subdue her husband, but Dan Snr

136

recovered faster than the couple anticipated. He threw himself against Jack and the two of them wrestled clumsily on the floor. Jack at least had the sense to throw the shotgun far out of his reach lest he accidentally discharge it into his father or wife. It skidded to a stop by the chair. Cassandra stood over them, adjusting her stance to avoid them when they rolled toward her. "Stop this! What is wrong with you two? Jack!"

The element of surprise quickly wore off for Dan Snr. He was already partially stunned by the shotgun stock, and Jack had gotten over the fact that he didn't hit his father hard enough. Jack twisted around him, cocked his arm back, fingers clenched, and socked his father in the jaw.

"Jack!" Cassandra held her arms out to stop him, but he'd already struck his father a third time, then a fourth. She tossed the revolver on the desk, grabbed Jack's shoulders, and heaved him off of his father. "That's enough!"

Jack shoved her back as gently as he could in the moment and threw himself back on his father, took hold of his shoulders, and dragged him toward the stairs. "Get up, old man."

Cassandra hesitantly touched his shoulder. "Jack…"

"Get up those stairs." Jack practically lifted his father up the first couple of steps. "Move it!"

Dan Snr barked over his hunched shoulder, "I'm going, you little shit!" Using the rail for support, Dan Snr made slow work of his ascension with Jack close behind him.

"Cass," Jack said, "Grab the guns."

Cassandra gathered the weapons and followed them upstairs, stealing one last, tentative glance at the glass box. She could have sworn something in it glanced back at her. She hurried up to the garage, slamming the door shut as quickly as she could pass through, and locked it. She followed her husband as he hustled Dan Snr alongside Wilma's car and up the stairs into the little foyer. She peered through the window in the garage door into the night and saw nothing. The driveway was lit. The trees beyond the frontline were dark. The snow appeared to be navy blue outside of the light's reach.

Dan Snr was stubborn at first. Jack

138

had to goad him into the foyer, attracting the others' attention. Wilma and Hannah entered through the other end of the foyer and greeted Dan Snr with cautious looks. They kept their distance as Jack pushed him into the kitchen.

"Sit," Jack barked.

His father obeyed, slumping in the chair with an elbow propped on the table. He looked through the picture window at the backyard and then eyed the videotape left near Marcy's apparently endless supply of wine.

Cassandra placed the guns on the island counter by the stove and took Jack's hand as he joined her behind it. He leaned over the counter, the pot lights in the ceiling casting harsh shadows over his eyes. He maintained a bitter glare toward his father, though by instinct his eyes occasionally scanned the backyard for intruders.

Wilma's eyes shifted between Jack and Dan Snr with concern and knowing frustration. "Were you two fighting?"

"He started it," Jack said. "Hand me the wine, will you, Marcy?"

"My wine now," Marcy replied, punctuating her refusal with a loud sip from her glass.

Scowling, Jack went into one of the overhead cabinets and took down an unopened bottle of red wine from 1995. He twisted the cork out with a loud *pop* and knocked it back straight from the bottle.

Wilma and Cassandra exchanged tired glances. Marcy drank quietly, glancing into the living room to see what the children were watching on the TV. Brian was glued to the screen, sitting far too close to the unit. Hannah was sobbing over her food, but Marcy felt too empty to comfort her daughter.

Cassandra leaned through the alcove to check on her own children. Harry and Martin were perched on the fireplace's hearth extension, their empty plates stacked beside Alistair, who was picking absently at his half-eaten dinner.

Dan Snr and Jack upheld their own private staring contest while the rest of the adults spectated in uncomfortable silence.

Dan Snr eventually broke it. "Well? I'm here, like you all wanted. Now what?"

Jack took a swig from the bottle. Set it on the marble countertop loudly. Cassandra cringed from the popping sound

140

it made. "I have half a mind to tie you to that chair."

"Rope's downstairs," Dan Snr shot back. "Oh, right. You don't want anyone down there."

"That's not the point."

"Then make it."

"You're gonna tell everyone what it is, exactly, you want to do. What you have in that fish tank."

"I want to protect everyone here, Jack, same as you."

"Your plan is unsound."

"Do you have something better? I'm all ears, kiddo."

Wilma entered the conversation, asking her husband, "What's downstairs? What is he talking about?"

"My research, honey," he replied. "The case. All the strange things that have been happening in these parts for the past three or four years. Maybe longer. This is just another footnote in an extensive textbook, as it were. I'm keeping a deterrent downstairs. Something that's keeping them at bay. They're too scared to come in—but they're also afraid of what might happen if they don't."

"What are you talking about?" Marcy asked.

Jack answered before his father could: "He thinks those jokers outside are connected to his research materials."

"They *are*."

"The two losers you chased off?" Marcy asked.

Cassandra said, "There're a lot more than two of them out there, now." This revelation sent Wilma and Marcy's heads swiveling toward the picture window. "We can't see them," Cassandra added. "They're hiding in the trees."

Dan Snr asked, "Haven't you been listening?"

Jack replied, "I think I've entertained that for as long as possible. The only thing I know for sure is that unnatural... *thing* you're keeping in the basement. That thing which I'm gonna destroy as soon as we're done having this conversation."

"You can't!"

"I'm not gonna listen to you go on and on about 'deterrence' anymore."

"God, for the final time, Wilma said irritably, "what's in the basement?"

Jack responded quickly: "Nothing

142

important. Just some weird thing Dad's been growing in his basement."

Dan Snr shot his son with a dirty look as the eyes of everyone who was out of the loop asked him silent questions. "The deterrence," he said slowly, "is the germination of what could be our only safe way out of here."

Marcy's eyebrows scrunched together in confusion. "The what?"

Jack oversimplified for his sister's benefit: "He's growing a demonic bitch out of his television set to scare off the cult that's got us surrounded from every direction."

Marcy leaned back in her chair. She peered into the woods again. "I don't see anybody."

Cassandra said, "There are cameras. We saw them hiding out in the woods with our own eyes."

Wilma said to her husband, "You installed cameras."

"Yes."

"When?"

"When I was putting up the Christmas lights."

"And you never thought to tell me

this?"

"I hoped I wouldn't have to. If I'd told you, you would've been even more concerned than you already were—"

"If you would have told me, I wouldn't have invited our children and grandchildren here!" she snapped at him. "And what's this about a 'demonic bitch in the basement'? There's a woman in the basement?" She approached her husband, tentatively, wary of his outburst toward their son, and what damage he could do to her should he have another one. "Daniel? *What* is going on, exactly?"

"There's little time to explain—"

"Try."

Dan Snr said. "We're in very real, very hopeless danger. I'm curating a way out for us all. Donna Anderson is growing. Even now, I feel so strange because of her."

"Strange *how*?" Wilma asked.

"She frightens them, Wilma. I know it."

"But how do you know?"

Jack cut in: "He *doesn't*."

"They're afraid of her."

"Who?" Wilma asked.

"The *people*!" Dan Snr growled,

144

startling Wilma. Jack stepped between his parents, but his father made no attempt to rise from his chair. "Why can't anyone in this fucking house just *listen* to me? They're here because of her. But they won't come in because of her. So long as we control her growth, they won't want to come in here and take us. But..." he suddenly lunged at Jack. Cassandra yelped. Wilma almost screamed. Marcy froze in her chair. Jack lurched away instinctively as his father latched onto his arm, fingernails digging into his sweater's sleeves. "*But* we need to watch them anyway. We can't let our guard down. Not for a minute. Not for a *second.*" His voice had lowered to a harsh, shuddering whisper. Jack could see real fear in his father's wide, glassy eyes. "And for God's sake, watch the children, too. *Watch them.*"

Marcy leaned back in her chair, allowing her a direct view of the living room. The children weren't sitting on the fireplace ledge anymore. Marcy wasn't concerned, yet. The TV was still playing behind the couch, which would obscure her view of all the children sitting in front of it. She stood up and took her wine glass over to the couch, and when she reached it she saw Harry, Martin, Alistair, and her own Brian and Hannah all sitting in a group far too close to the TV. Tears welled up in her eyes at the sight of her children. She knew she could only hope that John's death was sudden. The absence felt like a burning, rotting emptiness in the pit of her stomach. Every heartbeat was a jarring pang of grief. She could still see the burning wreckage. She could still see Deb twirling gracefully across a pool of blazing gasoline, a ballerina as the flames devoured her body. She could still hear Deb's horrible, choking laughter. A sound not unlike how she imagined a colony of night owls' overlapping shrieks from the trees would be. Deb had danced as John burned. Deb celebrated the deaths of her own husband and son. Child-like, monstrous glee even under pain of a fiery death. It was as if she hadn't noticed that she, too, was dying.

Marcy realized the kids had all turned around on the floor. They were staring at her. She hadn't noticed them moving. They weren't moving now.

"Is everything alright, Aunt Marcy?" Alistair asked.

146

Marcy forced a tight smile of reassurance. It wouldn't have convinced any adult, or teenager, but most of these kids were younger than that. "Yes. Everything's fine." She looked up at the TV and saw seemingly endless plains of golden wheat rippling with a silent breeze behind a wavering layer of visual static and light scratches in the picture. A figure seemed to be strolling along the horizon in the distance, nothing but a dark, blurry shape on the screen. The sky was a vast, grey, empty void threatening to descend and swallow everything, if it hadn't already started. Faint seagull shapes danced across the hollow horizon. "What're you watching?"

Before the children could answer, Cassandra leaned out of the kitchen doorway and around the grandfather clock. "How're the kids?"

"They're fine."

"Where's Dad, Mom?" Hannah asked. "Why did the cars explode?"

Marcy hesitated. "We'll be home soon. I'll tell you all about it later. Okay? Go watch TV." Hannah was watching her mother carefully, making a face that showed she knew something was wrong. *God, don't stare at me like that.* "Go," Marcy said.

"Okay." Hannah rejoined the others.

Marcy returned to the kitchen, fighting back tears. As she passed the grandfather clock, Westminster chimes rang out, startling her. She heaved a deep sigh, clutching her chest, her heart racing, as she went back to her chair in the corner. The gong followed, striking nine times. Three hours had passed seemingly in the blink of an eye. No one present could recall hearing it announce every quarter-hour since six.

After nine gongs that reverberated through the house, the grandfather clock went quiet, as did everyone else. There was nothing any of them wanted to talk about anymore, so they sat and listened to the static droning from the living room television and the ticking of the grandfather clock. The ticking seemed louder than usual.

Jack spotted something moving in the woods past the pond. He was about to say something about it when someone banged on the garage door.

148

Friday, December 15th, 2000 - Part VII

It was a startling noise that echoed through the house. No one moved after they'd turned their heads to stare down the narrow foyer. It was dark in there, but the garage's harsh light was filtered through the vertical, rectangular window in the door above the stairs. Anyone outside could easily look in through the square window in the outer door and see the freezer box right of the stairs to the foyer and Wilma's BMW parked to the left. If the light in the foyer was on, they would be able to see directly across to the closet where the coats were, as well as the window next to it overlooking the deck and the yard beyond it. They would be able to see that the kitchen light was on more clearly due to the foyer's lights being off.

Whoever knocked knew they were there.

"That must be the police," Wilma said, unable to hide the hopefulness in her voice.

Jack was quick with his rebuttal.

149

"But what if it isn't?"

"We called them ages ago."

"Yeah, but it could be someone else."

"The people who ran around the house, is that what you're implying?"

"That's exactly what I'm implying, Mom."

"And if it isn't?"

Dan Snr cut in: "It's not."

Wilma asked him, "How would you know? You can't see them from where you're sitting."

"We're being watched," Jack said, cocking his chin at the backyard.

Every head turned, every pair of eyes searched for what Jack saw in the forest.

Marcy said, "I don't see anything."

"Neither do I," Wilma said.

"They're there," Dan Snr said. "They've been there for hours. They know she's here. If they didn't, they would have stormed the house already, and we'd all be dead."

Jack sighed. He was getting tired of hearing that.

Another series of hard taps on the garage door set their heartrates up. A voice, deep and authoritative, call out

150

through two sets of doors: "O.P.P. I'm responding to a phone call about a disturbance."

"It *is* the police," Wilma exhaled with great relief. She started for the foyer, but Dan Snr leaped from his chair and blocked her exit.

"No. Don't."

"Dan, it's the police," Wilma said, trying to keep firm. "We're fine, now."

"We can't trust them. If only you saw for yourself what kind of people we're dealing with!" Dan Snr kept his arm and leg stretched across the doorway to keep his wife from passing. "Jack! You saw the horrific things they've done."

"I don't even know what I saw. Just a lot of horrible shit I wish I didn't see."

"We can't trust anyone but each other. The police... cannot... be trusted."

"Aren't they the ones who gave you all of those tapes in the first place?" Jack asked.

"Dan, *please*," Wilma said, trying to push by him. Her husband stood firm.

"Yes, that's correct. I don't know why they would do this to me. To test out a theory, maybe?"

151

Jack scoffed. "You really *are* crazy."

"Police department," their unseen visitor yelled through the door, "is anyone there?" They rapped their knuckles on the window again.

Cassandra was gripping Jack's arm tightly. Jack reached for the revolver. Dan Snr couldn't see where his son's hand was going due to the elevated ledge between them, but he hardly needed to guess. Slowly, calmly, Dan Snr raised his hand, the one that wasn't blocking Wilma's exit, and showed his palm to his son. "All I want is for us all to get through this night in one piece. The rest of us. Please, son. Marcy. Wilma. You *have got* to believe me. I know I haven't sounded like the most rational person lately, I understand that. But this is huge. This is big. It's big and it's got me scared. You should be scared too. We should all be scared."

"Why?" Cassandra asked.

"The police didn't help Cameron Morgan. In fact, they brought it back to him whenever it escaped him. Cameron Morgan was a cop once, too. I don't know exactly what part they have to play in all the strange goings-on around here, but the

152

connection between them is strong enough for my trust in them to be just about non-existent. From what little I have to actually go on, it started with the cops. And now you want to greet one standing right outside of our door."

They all heard the rattle of the doorknob as it echoed in the garage.

"Hear that?" Dan Snr asked them. He took his wife by the shoulders and gently guided her around the table, and pointed out the window into the blackness under the tree branches. "Look! They're out there."

Jack gripped the revolver. "Dad—"

"Throw me the camera. It's in the second drawer to your left."

After a moment, Jack decided to give him the benefit of the doubt. He let the revolver lie on the counter and went into the drawer closest to the grandfather clock. It was full of things like boxed staples, tape, paper, spare picture frames, a flashlight, and finally, a Pentax film camera with a 28-80mm lens attached to it. It looked too expensive to risk throwing across the room, but as he thought this, Dan Snr was turning off all the lights on the phalanx of switches by the kitchen exit. Before anyone could

153

ask why, he crossed the kitchen and thrust his hand over the counter. "The camera. Quickly."

Jack handed it to him without a word.

Dan Snr said to Cassandra, "Please take the children into the guest bedroom and don't come out until one of us say so."

Cassandra was about to protest, more out of confusion than anything else, but Jack said, "Let's do what he says for now, hon."

Cassandra hurried into the living room. Jack heard the children whine and moan in protest. He snarled impatiently, "Do what you're told!" The whining stopped, though a few exasperated sighs could still be heard as Cassandra herded them down the corridor. The TV was still on.

Dan Snr went to the window, stumbled against a chair leg on his way to the door. He unlocked it quietly, opened it, leaned out onto the deck, letting in cold winter air. He tinkered with the camera for a moment, furtively peeking over the barrier and glancing around as he did so. The driveway entrance was once again bombarded with another series of knocks,

154

which Dan Snr ignored as he squatted behind the balcony's waist-high perimeter wall.

Jack moved closer, joining Wilma and Marcy around the table.

Finally, the camera was set satisfactorily; Dan Snr raised it above the barrier and snapped a photograph of the backyard. A brief flash illuminated the trees beyond the pond and was reflected in at least a dozen pairs of tiny white orbs. Everyone gathered around the kitchen table saw faint shapes moving around, shapes that couldn't be defined as human from the brief visibility they had been allowed.

"Oh, my God," Marcy said, staring out into the forest, her eyes wide with fear.

Dan Snr scrambled back inside, shut the door, locked it. "I have to develop the film downstairs. We can keep an eye on Donna's progress in the meanwhile."

A figure suddenly appeared from around the garage and started up the steps. It was a man in a police uniform. He hobbled onto the deck, snow crunching, wood groaning under his feet, as he called out to them. "Hello? Anyone home?"

"Get down," Dan Snr whispered

under his breath.

Caught in the moment, everyone obeyed. Dan Snr helped his wife squat down due to her stiff knees. A moment later, a white beam of light penetrated the unlit kitchen, probing the darkness. They huddled together under the table. Marcy was holding her breath, gripping an empty wine glass.

The white beam disappeared, leaving only the faint blue light of the night filtering through the window, disturbed by a long, dark shadow that stretched across the floor and up one of the stools tucked under the bar counter. Snow rumbled softly with every step as the officer's feet packed it through the deck's seams. The shadow sprouted arms and raised them, cupping its hands against the sides of its face to block outside light from entering its peripherals as it pressed its face against the window. They could hear him breathing against the glass as he searched the dark interior of the house. He leaned away, wiped fog off the glass. The visitor shifted left, then right, toward the side door.

Someone giggled. Not in the house. Not on the deck. In the trees. The police officer's shadow froze in mid-step, remaining perfectly still across the white tiles on the kitchen floor. The group under the table watched the black outline of the visitor's head slowly turn until the side of his face could be defined by a pointed nose and tucked-in lower lip.

"Hello?" he called out.

A breeze whispered by, carrying unhinged titters with it. The shadow disappeared as the visitor went to the steps and headed for the pond. His voice was harder to discern the farther out he ventured. "Very funny. You have five seconds to show yourselves or I'm coming in there."

His command was met with shrill laughter from an unseen crowd. The house itself shuddered from the maniacal, animalistic howling, as did its occupants.

Marcy dropped her wine glass, clamped her palms over her ears, trembling. Her wine glass splintered on the floor.

Wilma froze, fingers rigid, face struck with terror.

Jack's doubt and anger gave way to a kind of primal fear that had him scurrying across the kitchen floor around the counter to retrieve the revolver he'd left on top. He grabbed the revolver, snatched up the shotgun and carried both back under the kitchen table. He handed the shotgun to his father. "Just in case."

Dan Snr nodded with grim understanding.

Jack willed his shaking legs to allow him enough strength to peer over the table and out into the backyard. He saw the cop standing lopsidedly by the pond shining his flashlight into the forest. Snow and ice glimmered like sheets of diamonds as his flashlight beams played over a hundred tree trunks and ice-coated bushes. "Hey!" the cop shouted at someone Jack couldn't see. "Stop!" He charged in pursuit of a shadow that darted across the trees, only to crash through the frozen surface of the pond. The things in the forest guffawed with lunatic mockery, louder than before.

"Shit," Jack hissed. He lunged for the door.

"No!" Dan Snr reached out to stop him.

"He fell in the pond," Jack said quickly, unlocking the door with clumsy fingers. He dropped the gun and it

158

crunched on top of Marcy's wine glass shards. He reached down to pick it up only to prick himself on glass. "Ah!" Jack reached down more carefully, picked up the revolver, went back to unlocking the door. "He'll freeze to death out there."

"Let 'im. He's one of them!"

"He doesn't seem to know who the hell they are any more than we do. I'm not gonna let him die in our backyard. Cover me."

Dan Snr was about to protest further when Jack got the door open and went out onto the deck. "Don't—shit! Jack! Goddamn it!" He gripped the shotgun with both hands and rushed into the cold after his son, who vaulted over the rail and trudged as quickly as he could through ankle-deep snow in the yard. "Jack! Get back here! It's too dangerous!"

The laughter hadn't subsided. It was all around them, escalating as their little show unfolded. They were entertained. Everything in Jack told him to turn back. *Turn back and run and hide. Leave the cop. Let him die. Save yourself.* Jack's sense of decency forced him to push through it. Too many people have died

159

tonight already. Good people. A cop was drowning and freezing to death for doing his job.

"Run," someone in the forest jibed. "Run, run! Faster!"

He fired a warning shot into the upper branches of the trees. A scream cut through the laughter and then the forest fell completely silent, except for the desperate thrashing of the cop's limbs in the pond. Jack reached the pond, chanced two more seconds glancing at the woods around him as he tucked his revolver in the waistband of his jeans in the small of his back. Braced his right foot against a sturdy rock and bent forward, took hold of one of the cop's arms and pulled as hard as he could. The pond's freezing water splashed on him, felt like icicles had pierced through his clothes with instant numbing cold. He shivered as he dragged the cop out. He could feel them watching. They could rush him. All of them at once would be unstoppable. The cop wouldn't stand a chance. Neither would he, no matter how good he and his father were with their firearms. Even so, Jack had never shot a human being before. He wasn't sure if he could. Before tonight,

160

he hadn't even aimed a firearm at another person.

The cop gagged and sputtered on his hands and knees. His flashlight was gone.

"Come on," he told the cop, unable to hide the tremble in his voice. His eyes scanned the bushes behind the pond, the closest point at the edge of the forest. The darkness of the trees seemed to inch closer.

"Get up. Get up." Jack took hold of the man's longer arm and half-dragged him back across the yard toward the house.

"He's not coming in here," Dan Snr shouted from the deck.

"He's freezing to death," Jack yelled back. "He needs help."

"He *is not* coming in here."

The cop leaned against Jack as he staggered, struggling to keep up, nearly falling more than once as Jack pulled him back up. Clumps of snow stuck to them as they slogged through it. It seemed to get heavier, thicker, resisting their escape. Their backs were wide open to whatever threat hung around, while Dan Snr continued to dispute their approach from the deck.

"One more step and I'll shoot him! I

161

mean it!"

"Dan!" Wilma's shout was almost shrill, high enough to startle both husband and son. "That's enough. Jack, bring him inside in front of the fireplace."

"Wilma, we can't—"

Wilma jabbed a long forefinger in his direction. "*You* can get your ass back inside, too, before I change my mind and leave you out here with whatever's running around in my garden."

Dan Snr gave her a pleading look. He had completely faltered now, all sense of bravado gone.

"Don't think I'm bluffing," Wilma said icily.

Jack brought the cop inside, not without a sour exchange of looks between himself and his father. He brought the man, who was now convulsing violently from the cold, into the living room in front of the fireplace. It was gas, turned way up, emitting a pulsing heat that was both comforting and overwhelming. Just as a precaution—either due to his father's paranoia rubbing off on him or his own uncertainty of the entire situation, he couldn't be sure—Jack took the cop's gun

162

and his Taser in their holsters by unclipping them from his belt. The cop protested, but was unable to get a solid word through his chattering teeth. He also took the man's pepper spray and clipped them to his own belt.

"You'll get these back when we're sure you're not a threat."

The cop tried to mouth a response, but his violent tremors prevented him from speaking coherently. Jack knew he wasn't too thrilled on the prospect.

Wilma came out of the guest room with a change of clothes for the cop. After the cop had a chance to warm up, they guided him to the bathroom to take a hot shower and change into dry clothes.

"How are Cassandra and the kids?" Jack asked his mother.

"They're doing alright. A little frightened."

"We all are."

Marcy was refilling a new glass at the table, glancing constantly out the window with newfound paranoia. Dan Snr sat across from her, staring into the backyard, unmoving, unblinking, obsessive, with the shotgun laid across his lap.

163

Wilma took a seat on the couch. Jack remained by the fireplace, watching her. He glanced briefly at the television, at an undulating, golden wheat field under a swirling grey sky before it cut abruptly to cute polar bears drinking Coca-Cola straight from the bottle.

Wilma was staring sullenly at the floor.

"You okay, Mom?" Jack asked, his voice barely a whisper.

Wilma shook her head. "I suppose I'm just... a little overwhelmed."

"Me, too, Mom."

"Why do you have that police officer's weapons on your belt?"

"It's for our protection."

"Against the *police*?" Wilma was incredulous. "You've been spending too much time with your father tonight."

"I hate to admit it, Mom, but he's been right almost every step of the way. Even if he *is* crazy. Taking that cop's weapons keeps risks low for everybody. Including him. If he's armed, Dad just might have the right excuse to shoot him. Unarmed, he stands a better chance at gaining our trust. Dad won't shoot an

164

unarmed man."

"I didn't think your father had it in him to pistol-whip his son, either," Wilma said dryly, "but I suppose that proves what I really know. How does your head feel?"

"Tylenol kicked in a while ago. I'll be fine. I'm gonna go check on Cass and the kids."

"Okay."

Jack left the kitchen. He slowed his pace as he passed through the living room and connected foyer, the ticking of the grandfather clock loud in his left ear. He glanced at the front door, at the decorative stained glass tiles that bordered it. He maintained his slow pace as he went by the bathroom to make sure water was still splashing in there. Meant the cop was actually in the shower and not just running the water to deceive them. He progressed further down the corridor, passing framed family photos toward the master bedroom on the left, laundry room at the very end, and the guest room on the right. The guest room was the only room with its door closed. Jack leaned into the master bedroom. Two windows looking out into the driveway flanked the king-sized bed.

He peered through both windows and studied the trees. He could see shapes prowling around in there, smooth surfaces dully reflecting the powerful light illuminating the gravel lot.

Just then, something small, white, and round flew up out of the trees and landed on the roof. Jack waited, deciding to observe their activity a little longer to assess the threat. Eventually, another projectile arced upward from between two birches, but this one fell short and plonked on the edge of the drive. A snowball. They were throwing snowballs at the house.

Jack felt like laughing. If they were so bored, why didn't they just leave?

He left the bedroom and turned into the laundry room. Two French doors, sealed against the cold, provided an alternate exit to the front yard. Without turning on a light, Jack crossed the room and peered through the windows. He gripped one of the handles and tested it.

The French doors opened. Cold air penetrated his clothes.

Jack's heart plummeted into his stomach. He could have sworn these doors were locked. God. They had a way in this

166

entire time. He frantically searched around the dark laundry room, looking for anything out of the ordinary, anything that may not belong, anything that may be hidden in the shadows, in plain sight if he'd just switched the light on. He shut the doors and turned the lock. Tested the doors again, tugging hard. The French doors rattled quietly, secure.

Jack drew the revolver from his waistband and scanned the laundry room again, squinting at every shadow. He looked down at the floor, at the path outside through the French doors' windows. The only footprints he could see were the ones belonging to the first intruder he pursued, as well as his own footprints going into the front yard and then the bushes lining the property's edge. No fresh ones mingled with the old ones, as far as he could tell. The pinewood floor was also dry and had recently been mopped clean. Recently... he switched on the light, then began his search for the mop and bucket. He checked the closet by the dryer. The mop was in the bucket in the corner beside a box of dryer sheets and a few bottles of detergent and stain remover. Jack felt the inside of the

167

bucket. It was dry, thus it hadn't been used *too* recently. Since the light was on, he gave the floor another look for footprints. There were none. Relief washed through him like a cold drink on a hot day. He drew the blinds over the French doors, turned off the light, and knocked on the guest room door.

"Cass, it's Jack."

Cassandra opened the door and stood so that Jack couldn't look in. When she saw it was truly him, she widened the gap in the door, lunged out, and hugged her husband tightly. "Jesus, Jack," she whispered.

Jack could see the children had all piled into the bed. Alistair and Harry were fast asleep. Martin was muttering sleepily to himself, as he often did, trying to stay awake. Brian sat cross-legged on the floor in front of the window, staring out into the front yard. Hannah sat on the bed, her legs dangling over the side. Being the oldest child there, she was the most aware of what was going on, but was still confused about the specifics. One look at her face and Jack could tell—she knew her father, her youngest uncle, one of her aunts, and her

168

cousin Marcus were all dead.

Cassandra drew away from him. Jack cocked his head toward Brian. "Is he okay?"

Cassandra gave a small chuckle. "He's taking first watch. He must've seen someone trying to sneak up to the house once before."

"Did he say that?"

"He implied it, but he wouldn't say anything else."

Jack asked Hannah, "Are you okay, kiddo?"

"Dad's dead, isn't he?"

Taken aback by his niece's bluntness, Jack felt resigned to be the bearer of bad news. "Yes," he said softly, "he had an accident."

"They're all dead."

"Yeah," Jack said, sitting on the bed next to her. "They're all dead. Life does that to you sometimes."

"We're all going to die, aren't we?"

"No," he said. "We're not going to die."

"How do you know?"

"Because I'll protect you and your Aunt Cass will protect you, and so will your mom and grandparents. We're all protecting you right now."

Cassandra came over, knelt down in front of Hannah, and took her small hand in both of hers. "We're not gonna let anything happen to you, okay? I promise."

"Then why are we still here? I wanna go home."

"We'll take you home soon," Cassandra assured her. "Try to relax and get some sleep. I'll be right here with you."

"Promise?"

"I promise, sweetie. Lie down. Try to get some sleep. You, too, Brian. Get into bed, now."

"But I'm keeping watch," Brian protested, turning his pouting lower lip over his shoulder toward Cassandra.

Cassandra went around the bed and tousled his hair. "It's my turn to keep watch, little man. If I see anything, you'll be the first to know. Okay?"

He nodded. "Okay."

"Hop in, now." She switched on a nightlight plugged into the wall. "With light comes the absence of monsters."

Brian obeyed, crawling into bed and tucking himself into the other end, his feet brushing between Alistair's and Harry's. His head sunk into a spare pillow.

Hannah allowed Jack to tuck her in on the other side of the bed with a barrier of pillows erected between her and the boys. Jack kissed her forehead good night.

"You too, Uncle Jack."

Cassandra took Jack's hand and led him into the hall. Jack waited a moment to make sure the water was still splashing in the bathroom. Then he asked her, "You gonna be okay?"

"I'll be fine. Just... you know, maybe your dad's wrong. Maybe we should just pack the kids into your mom's car and make a break for it."

"I'm on the fence about it. I saw a few of them throwing snowballs on the other side of the driveway."

"God." She shuddered. "What do they *want* with us?"

"I don't know, hon. Look, I gotta go take care of something. Here. Take this." He handed her the officer's Beretta.

"Jack—"

"Don't open this door unless it's me."

"But Jack—"

"Remember, red means dead. Just in

171

case, okay?"

"Jack, this is crazy."

"Nothing we can do about it now."

"What about Marcy?"

"I don't know. She's drunk and she's been acting weird."

"Jesus, Jack…"

He rubbed her shoulders, trying to be reassuring. She stared at the wall, looking defeated. "We'll be okay. Hey." He framed her face in his hands, gently raised her head up so she could see the truthfulness behind his next statement: "The minute things get out of hand, we're outta here. Okay?"

The frown on her face told him she was unconvinced. "Things are *already* out of hand, Jack."

"Worse. We can handle this." He kissed her. "I love you. I'll be back."

"I love you, too," she murmured, but he'd already started back toward the kitchen. She watched him disappear around the corner and then closed the guest room door behind her.

The children were in bed. She switched off the light. Only the deep blues and purples filtering through the window,

172

as well as the faint glow of the nightlight in the opposite corner; provided her with visibility. She felt a few of the children looking at her as she crossed to the rocking chair by window. "Close your eyes."

She sat down and studied the gun in her hands, turned it over a few times, rubbed the oil residue between her thumb and fingers. She'd seen many movies and had been given a demonstration once before on gun safety. The safety was switched on. She pulled the slide back and saw a brass glint in the chamber. She ejected the magazine and checked its capacity. Full. She quietly slid it back in, secured it with a soft, satisfying click. She inhaled deeply and sighed, deciding to keep the gun on her lap. She could hear the shower running, but barely. If the cop decided to make a break for the guest room, for whatever reason, she wasn't sure if she'd have the courage to shoot him. The gun was as reassuring as it wasn't. Self-defense? Perhaps. But shooting a cop in this country would be a hard thing to justify, no matter the reason.

Cassandra sat in the darkness and waited.

Friday, December 15th, 2000 - Part VIII

"Dust," it croaked as it shuffled through snow drifts, crunching ice and stiff branches under its charred feet. "Ashes." It was seemingly surrounded by ash. It could see embers no one else would be able to see.

No. Light. Artificial light. Up ahead, a dull yellow glow burned through a phalanx of frozen birch trees. It stood there, mesmerized by the glow. Then it pressed forward, teetering dangerously to one side, then the other, as it instinctively followed the light.

"To ashes."

"Cameron?" a woman called from the trees.

It halted.

"Is that you?"

It turned, greeted by a television that sat perched on a fallen maple, its cord extending all the way toward the strange glow in the near distance. A woman's face flickered on the screen. She seemed to be peering through it as if it were a window.

174

"Are you there?"

It approached the TV, closing the gap between them with greater urgency than ever before. It vaulted forward, collapsing on its hands and knees. Its weakened frame threatened to come apart from the fall, but with a shudder and a moment of pause, it decided it was still safe to move. It reached for the television.

"It *is* you," the woman cried happily.

It said, "Maureen."

"There's something I need you to do, Cameron. Can you do that for me?"

"Muh... Maureen."

She held her arms through the screen. "Come to me, Cameron. Come to me."

"Maureen." It reached for her. Frozen maggots dropped out of the open gash in its forearm. As its hand drew closer to hers, her hands drifted a little further out of its reach. The thing crawled closer to the television. Her hands returned through the screen. Maureen giggled playfully, turned, and leaped through a field of tall yellow wheat, twirling like a ballerina.

"Dust." It took hold of the edge of the screen, its fingers hooking through it. It pulled itself through the small window and

175

entered the field. "Maureen." Its empty sockets followed Maureen with strange, instinctual longing, as if the thing didn't know why it had been roaming so aimlessly until now.

"Come on, Cameron. Run with me." She pranced through the tall grass that lined a sandbar. Beyond it was an ocean, its foamy waves rolling in with deafening roars. The water was green and blue and everything in between, shimmering, reflecting sunlight that wasn't there. The sky above was the colour of concrete on a rainy day. A humid summer breeze swept through the tall grass, thawing the icy stiffness from the thing's joints.

This place wasn't natural, but the thing didn't care. Maureen spun in a bright white dress, drifting weightlessly through the tall grass surrounded by an ethereal aura. She looked like an angel. The thing was drawn to her, a moth to an old flame.

"Maureen." Decaying joints groaned as it pursued her. Black skin shavings fluttered from its thin frame as it strained to keep up. She was always out of its grasp. It pushed forward, desperate to have her again.

176

"Come on, Cameron! Follow me!" She clasped her hands behind her back, arms straight, and waited for him to get within a few feet of her before leaping ahead again.

If the thing that was once a man were alive, it would have been frustrated. Perhaps it would have given up, cursed and swore, and went back. Instead it pressed on with single-minded determination. "Maureen." Nothing else mattered.

*

Shortly after the grandfather clock announced half past nine, the bathroom door opened. Jack and Dan Snr met with the police officer, now dressed in loose sweatpants and a fleece sweater, at the end of the corridor where the front door could provide a quick exit. They had him sit down at the dining room table. Wilma offered him tea, coffee, and hot chocolate— he chose hot chocolate—and while she was preparing that, the officer gave Jack and Dan Snr an expectant look. "My gear?"

"We'll hold on to it for now," Dan Snr said quickly. "We're feeling a little paranoid tonight."

The officer remained completely

calm, resting his left elbow on the table while keeping his right hand on his thigh. "It's a felony to take an officer's gun."

"It's a felony to impersonate a police officer, too," Dan Snr replied coolly.

"I *am* a police officer."

"Where's your nametag?"

"Should be on my uniform."

"Badge?"

"Same place."

"Go check."

It took Jack a moment to realize Dan was talking to him. "Check yourself."

Dan Snr sighed and walked heavily into the bathroom. Jack maintained eye contact with the officer, even as Wilma came around with a steaming mug of hot chocolate topped with marshmallows. They heard clothes rustling and a few things clattering about, and then Dan Snr re-joined them at the second table. "Looks legitimate enough."

"I thought so, too," the officer said.

"So, Officer Henry Jameson." Dan Snr pulled the chair at the other end of the table out, nearly bumping it against the buffet and hutch, and sat down. The shotgun was once again resting across his

178

lap. "What did you see out there?"

"I'm gonna need my radio."

"What for?"

"Call for backup. There're too many of them out there."

"Did you see them? Clearly?"

"Not exactly."

"What's that supposed to mean? You either saw them or you didn't."

"Oh, I *saw* them, alright. But they weren't like anything I've seen before."

"Elaborate."

Officer Jameson shrugged. With a look of helplessness, he sipped his hot chocolate and wiped marshmallow cream from his upper lip. For a while, he held the mug in both hands, staring at the floor. Then, he said, "They sounded human. They didn't *look* like any humans I know. Probably just a bunch of assholes in weird costumes. We've been getting a lot of those lately."

"The motel," Dan Snr said.

Officer Jameson nodded. "That was the biggest one, I think. And the worst."

"What do you know about Donna Anderson?"

"Donna Anderson?" Recognition

179

flashed across Officer Jameson's face for a moment. "The name rings a bell."

"Mother of two. Husband went missing. Kids were found dead in the basement of their house. Rumour has it her son had something to do with a string of home invasions and assaults around the neighbourhood."

"I can't confirm or deny these things. Nothing's been proven, except the fact that people have been dying. Kids've gone missing, too. The ones that *aren't* killed."

"Didn't you watch the videotapes?"

"I'm not a detective. I haven't seen anything." Officer Jameson sipped his hot chocolate, enjoyed it, and then waved his free hand with exasperated helplessness before sipping his drink again. He swallowed and said, "So, feel free to ask me more questions for which I don't know the answers to."

"What *do* you know?"

"Not much. Just rumours. People talk. The station hasn't really been the same since the first wave."

"'The first wave'?" Jack asked.

"Assaults," Officer Jameson said. "Look, even if I knew more about the case,

180

I'm not at liberty to discuss it with civilians. All I know is that we're all stuck inside this house and that we're surrounded by a small group of hooligans with a sick sense of humour—and I don't have my gun. Or pepper spray."

"You'll get those back when we know we can trust you," Dan Snr replied flatly.

"I'm a *cop*," Officer Jameson exclaimed, "you're supposed to trust me."

"You saw the wreck outside, correct? You must have." Dan Snr waited for Officer Jameson to nod his head in confirmation. "That was caused by one of our own. She was fine before, but then, for whatever reason, she ran out there and caused some other family members we were expecting later to crash. Easy enough mistake to make, I guess, if you've the mind of a six-year-old, which Deborah did not. Then she set the wreck—and herself—on fucking fire."

A teacup shattered on the floor. Wilma collapsed on her knees.

"Mom?" Jack went to her aid.

"I'm sorry," she said. "I'll be okay."

"Let me clean this up for you."

"No, I've got it. It's okay."

"Sit down, Mom. I got it." Jack guided her to the chair by the foyer. "Keep an eye on that backyard for us, okay? I'll clean this up."

While Jack retrieved the broom and dustpan, Dan Snr continued, his voice a quieter tone. "Four of us are already dead without a conceivable explanation. It only took a lighter. The last thing I want is for the same thing to happen again, but this time with a gun in the hands of a stranger. Cop or not."

Officer Jameson watched him for a beat, processing what he'd been told. "Okay," he said, "fair enough. But if whoever's out there decides it's too cold outside, I want my gun back."

Dan Snr's fingers tapped a quick, impatient rhythm across the wooden stock of his shotgun. "We'll see." He leaned forward, planting both feet firmly on the floor, and stood up to his full height. By this time, Jack had just finished disposing of the teacup's pieces in the garbage bag under the kitchen sink, and was just stepping through the alcove into the dining area. Father and son looked at each other over the island counter. "Watch him. I'm

182

going downstairs."

Jack watched him leave without a word.

Officer Jameson finished his hot chocolate, and set the mug down on a foam coaster on the table. He'd been staring at Jack for a while now, reading him in ways Jack couldn't figure yet.

"You don't believe him, do you?" Officer Jameson asked.

"What?"

"Your old man. You don't believe him."

"About what, exactly?"

"You think you're all going about this all wrong, don't you?"

"Maybe we are, maybe we aren't."

"You have kids here, don't you?"

Jack's eyes narrowed slightly, though he tried to hide his emotions. His grip on the cop's Beretta tightened. His finger slid a quarter of an inch off the trigger guard. "How do you know that?" Jack asked slowly.

"Your mom called for help. Said there were kids here."

Jack relaxed, ever-so-slightly. "So what's your point?"

"No point, really. I just find it strange that their parents wouldn't try to take them and run the second they found out about those prowlers out there."

Jack said nothing. Just glared at him. Waiting for the hook.

"Is it your old man? Seems he's running the show. He's got the biggest gun. He's the one giving orders. The children, they're hidden away, aren't they? In a bedroom or the basement. He won't let anyone leave."

"If you've got a point, I suggest you make it."

Jameson showed his palms. "Just stating an observation, that's all."

"Well, state it in your head. I'm not interested in hearing what you have to say."

"Why's that?"

"My dad might be nuts, but he's been more-or-less correct since the beginning. And right now, it's really starting to look like he was right about bringing you in from the cold."

"Easy, man. I'm not a threat to you. I'm just making observations. Given my position, you can see that, right?"

"I can see just fine from where I'm

184

sitting."

"Look—we're on the same side. I just wanna get everyone out of harm's way. If I could just go to the car and radio for backup, we can deal with our mutual problem and get everyone to safety. Sounds logical, right?"

"Under normal circumstances, I'd agree with you. But I've seen too much weird shit tonight to just give you your way, cop or no cop. Let *me* state an observation."

Jameson maintained a casual demeanour as he replied, "Hell, by all means."

"Your station outsourced all these weird videotapes and documents to my dad to help with the investigation."

"I'm not directly involved in it."

"So you've said. But when my mom called your dispatcher, they sent you."

"So?"

"So why wouldn't they send someone who knew more about this? Someone who knew that my dad was going through the files?"

"I couldn't tell ya. The dispatchers aren't involved in the investigation, either.

They get a distress call, they send the next available unit. End of story. It feels like you're scraping for a conspiracy that isn't there."

"Maybe," Jack admitted, "or maybe I'm just being cautious."

"Like your old man?"

"Yeah, but less crazy."

Jameson chuckled. "Of course."

They fell silent. Jameson glanced through the window into the backyard, but didn't see anything other than trees and snow.

Jack didn't move.

Marcy spilled some wine on her lap and hissed, "Shit."

Wilma strode over to the dining room table and asked, "Anyone want another drink?"

"I'm good, thanks," said Officer Jameson, turning away from the window.

"Jack?"

"No thanks, Mom."

Wilma re-entered the kitchen and said quietly to Marcy, "You should drink some water, hon."

"I don't want to." Marcy was still very coherent, but her movements were

186

sluggish and she was struggling to stay awake.

"I really think you should, sweetie."

"I disagree. Shove off, Mom."

"Okay. Okay." Wilma sighed and took a seat by the foyer entrance.

Officer Jameson asked Jack, "Hey, you ever follow what happened in Texas a few years back? Waco?"

"Seriously? Gonna play that card now? We're not cultists. We're just scared. Scared and cautious. Right now we don't even know whether we can trust you or not. Especially since it took you hours to get here. No fire truck, no ambulance, or multiple units. Just one man. You. I don't know about you, but to me, that sounds kinda suspicious. Mom reported four deaths in our driveway. Right, Mom?"

"Yes," she answered from across the room. Now it was her turn to fill a glass with wine, emptying what was left in Jack's bottle.

"So you can just sit right there. Without a radio."

Officer Jameson leaned back in his chair with a frown on his face. "And if I don't? What if I just leave?"

"Then leave. And don't come back until you have that backup you were talking about."

"Can I have my gun back?"

"No."

"I'm not going out there without my gun."

"That sucks."

"You know—"

"Yeah, yeah, it's a crime to take a police officer's gun. I really don't care. Given the circumstances, I think your chief will understand. That's if you've actually got one."

"Are you implying I'm a phony cop?"

"Badge, gear, gun, they don't really mean anything to me right now."

"Because your dad said so."

"No. Because my instincts say so. You're chiming some weird bells right now and I don't like it. You're more than welcome to go out the same door you came in anytime. But you're leaving without anything you can use as a weapon." Jack was stiff as a board, struggling to keep himself from faltering under Jameson's gaze, which was becoming less friendly with every spoken word. "I have a family

188

to protect. I'm sure you can respect that."

Jameson's eyes softened. He smiled in a way that was supposed to emulate friendliness. It made Jack shudder instead. "I don't agree with it, but I understand it. How's that?"

"It'll have to do," Jack said.

Friday, December 15th, 2000 - Part IX

The grandfather clock struck the hour. Ten gongs howled through the house, echoing down the corridor to the guest room where the children, most of them asleep on the water bed, stirred. Cassandra was slumped in a rocking chair by the dresser, on top of which a panoramic mirror reflected the entire room within its frame, including the back of Cassandra's head. She'd fallen asleep while she was watching over them. The air in the room was chill.

Hannah was the only one awake. She was watching shadows dance on Cassandra's sleeping face across the room, distorting her features into dark pits and a crooked smile that frightened her. *Just your imagination playing tricks on you,* her mother often told her, and sometimes she saw reason and believed that to be true.

Tonight, however, the Rorschach smile persisted. Usually it darted across the room, following wherever Hannah's eyes went and manifesting again in the darkest place in her line of sight. It never left

190

Cassandra's face. Ink blotches wriggled intricately along the edges of Cassandra's face; her eyes appeared to be melting with the upward curves of her demonic smile. Hannah began to suspect that the shadows would take control of Aunt Cassandra's entire body and shoot at her, her cousins, and her brother with the revolver Uncle Jack had given her.

Aunt Cassandra stirred suddenly. Hannah's heart leaped in terror. *She's gonna do it,* she thought. *She's gonna kill us.*

It was a crazy idea; Hannah knew that. Cassandra was always nice to them and never treated them like a hindrance, unlike Uncle Jack or even their own parents. And with her father dead, Mom would be too preoccupied with her own grief at his passing to pay much attention to her children. Hannah had a feeling she and Brian would have to start taking care of themselves and each other.

Brian was more inward than usual today. Hannah knew he knew but she didn't say anything. She didn't want to upset him. She wasn't sure what he thought about it. He probably just wanted to look

191

strong, stronger than he really was. Even while he slept, he was turning over and muttering, his cheeks wet with tears and perspiration from a nightmare.

Hannah slid out from under the covers, timing her movements carefully as the water bed bobbed and sloshed under her. She climbed over Brian and hopped silently onto the floor. She watched the ink blotches distorting Aunt Cassandra's face fade away as she approached her.

She stood by Cassandra, who continued to sleep soundly, and looked out the narrow window that was taller than her. Through it, she could see the trees standing in the front yard, still and black and silent against the snow. The road beyond them was deserted, concealed behind snowbanks erected by the local plowing company. There were no lights, only the faint blue glow of the moon reflecting on twinkling white dunes formed by wind and footprints. Occasionally the overhead branches were disturbed; weird shapes stretched and darted in all directions across the snow.

Hannah watched the branches dance in silence. Something banged above the ceiling. A low rumble filled the room as

192

packed snow cascaded down onto the path. Hannah kept her eyes up, watching the eavestrough shake off a few thin icicles—the rest of them wiggled, clinked together as something shuffled above Hannah's line of sight. More snow spilled over and plummeted onto the path, as well as a pair of icicles that had managed to hold on to their perches until they were displaced by two black, frostbitten fingers. Hannah's skin crawled as she watched more fingers curl under the eavestrough. Something larger and rounder started to reveal itself from above. She quickly ducked away from the window and pressed her back against the wall beside it. The thing's shadow descended the column of light that shone across the floor toward her, a black silhouette of elongated, humanoid proportions. The shadow's long arms reached down to the path as long tendrils, while its head was shaped more like a pumpkin that had been smashed in.

Hannah realized too late that the tall mirror on the other side of the room had given away her position to the thing in the window. From its vantage point, she was perfectly framed within the mirror's reflection. She, in turn, could see the thing more clearly, but due to the light on its back, she couldn't make out any details on its front.

"Hannah," it whispered through the window, fogging up the glass with its heavy, rasping breaths. "Hannaaaahhhhh."

Hannah was too frightened to move or speak. Something had her caught in a vise. Her muscles failed her. Her vocals tightened up. Her eyes welled with tears that wouldn't come. She was as rooted to her spot as any of the trees outside were anchored to the lawn.

"It's Daddy, baby," said the thing outside. "It's okay to let me in. I survived the crash. See? I'm okay." A white slit appeared in the black void under the thing's hood. Hannah could feel it staring at her through its reflection. It had no pupils and it did not blink. "Is Brian with you? What about Jack and Cass's boys? Hannah? I know you're in there. I can see you."

Hannah trembled as an unexplainable terror took hold of her. Her eyes burst with tears. She blubbered, almost incoherently, "Go away!"

"Hannah." John's voice lowered an

octave, stern and commanding, "Open this window. You open this window right now, Hannah. Or I'll have to punish you. Hannah. Hannaaaaahhhhh. Open this window. It's too cold out here, I forgot my coat. You wouldn't want daddy to freeze his butt off, would you?"

Hannah pressed her hands over her ears and slid to the floor, hiding behind the bed. The thing claiming to be her father couldn't see her in the mirror anymore.

"Come out, Hannah. Come out. Come out."

"You're dead," Hannah cried. "You're dead. You're dead. You're dead!"

"I'm not dead!" Its voice was hushed, but it was snarling now, barely containing the volume of its rage. It didn't want to wake Cassandra or the other children. "Let me in." An inhuman growl clawed its way out of the charred depths of its throat. "Open this window, you little bitch! Why do I always have to tell you the same things thousands of times before you finally fucking *do it*?!" It lost its temper and pounded its palm flat on the window.

Cassandra started in the chair, lurching forward with the instinctive

195

reaction to falling. "God!" She looked around the room, caught sight of Hannah curled up against the wall. "Oh, Hannah, baby, what's wrong?" She rose up clumsily from the rocking chair, using the dresser for support, and glimpsed something in the corner of her eye. A long black shadow on the floor, something unfamiliar and shapeless. Her eyes followed it to the window. She turned and stared into the eyes of John's face, or a grim parody of it, encrusted in bubbled layers of dried blood and melted flesh, his eyes pure white and bulging from clotted sockets. His skull was misshapen, curved inward on the left side. He had no left ear. The skin and cartilage of his nose had burned away, revealing a jagged black pit in the center of his face. His lips were nonexistent, revealing blackened teeth. Its eyes burned bright with rage. Like a poor imitation of a bat, it pulled itself up and out of sight onto the roof.

Cassandra stood frozen in shock. Her bulging eyes twitched involuntarily as tears streamed down her face. Her mouth hung open. A scream caught in her throat.

High-pitched tittering rang out from

196

the trees and hung in the air long after it stopped. On any other day, Cassandra might have thought it to be the call of some strange bird.

The ceiling groaned rhythmically as the thing's hands and feet bombarded the roof, packing snow down, making as much noise as it could. Its thunderous, crunching pitter-patter woke the children. Cassandra heard questions, but couldn't process them. She heard only *its* ceaseless bombardment; a rapid heartbeat drumming in her ears that shook her to her core.

She whispered, "No."

With the gun tucked in her sweater pouch, Cassandra dragged the kids out of bed and ordered them to follow her. She herded them into the living room, much to the confusion of her husband, in-laws, and guest. She said to Jack, "We're leaving."

"Whoa, whoa." He raised his hands. "What're you doing, Cass?"

"I'm taking the kids out of here. Don't try to stop me." She took in the cop's appearance and decided to keep him within her peripherals as Jack tried to get in front of her.

Marcy was slumped over the table

and not stopping anyone.

Wilma watched the children file by her into the foyer as Cassandra ordered them to get their coats, mitts, hats, and boots on. She seemed completely unsurprised by this turn of events.

Jack took her arm. "Cass—"

She yanked her arm away. "I can't stay here. I'm sure as hell not leaving the kids here, either. I'm going. I can't do this anymore."

"What happened? Cass?" He reached for her hand again, instinctively, more out of confusion than a need to keep her from leaving.

"Don't. I can't. I *saw* him, Jack."

"Who?"

"John." Cassandra nearly broke into tears. "I saw John."

Jack was utterly perplexed. "What?"

"Where's the body? Did you see the body? Didn't you see him in the wreck? He burned, right? Where's the body, Jack?"

"I didn't pull him out of the wreck, Cassandra, it was on fire!"

"I *saw* him, Jack!"

"What do you mean, you saw him?

198

He's dead!" Jack was shouting now. "He's *dead*, Cassandra! Just like the others! They're *all dead*!"

"Then why, when I looked out the window, did I see him? He looked *right at me*, Jack."

Jack turned his head toward Wilma, who'd gone completely pale. The kids were zipping up their coats and thumping their boots on the floor as they slid their feet into them. Hannah was sobbing. He turned back to Cassandra, his eyes narrow with confusion and worry. He tried to speak, but words failed him. He and Officer Jameson exchanged confused glances, though Officer Jameson seemed to be strangely calm in his chair, more intrigued than frightened.

Cassandra tried to go around Jack, but he stopped her. "Let go of me."

"Wait, Cass."

"I said, let go!"

"Wait! What did he... did he look like John?"

"What the fuck kind of question is that? Of course it *looked* like John! It *sounded* like John! But those eyes... his eyes were different. I... I can't describe it!

199

I won't. Get out of my way, Jack."

"I can't let you go out there."

"Give me the keys. I'm taking the car." She asked Wilma, "Where are the keys?"

"Cass, don't." Jack tugged on her arm. When she pulled away, he grabbed her again. "We don't know what they'll do once you're out there!"

"So I'll floor it! Let go of me!" Cassandra shoved him away.

Wilma said, calmly, "The keys are hanging by the door."

"*Mom*!" Jack exclaimed.

Wilma looked tired, resigned to some unspoken fate. "Jack. If she has a chance to get the children out to safety, I'll allow it. You're starting to sound like your father."

Jack bristled.

Cassandra didn't look at him. She went into the foyer and grabbed the keys off the hook.

Officer Jameson began to rise. Jack whirled and pointed at him. "You stay right there. Don't move."

Jameson lowered himself back into his chair and showed his palms in surrender. His expression and body

200

language was indifferent, almost callously so. "I didn't even do anything."

"I don't care. Just sit right there and keep your hands where we can see them."

"Can I say something first?"

Jack barked, "*What*?"

"They're coming." Officer Jameson pointed toward the backyard. Everyone instinctively turned their heads toward the nearest window and saw for themselves an approaching assemblage of humanoid oddities shambling toward the house in a wide, shrinking circle.

All of them were dressed tightly in black leather, electrical tape, or spandex. They carried heavy electronic equipment on their backs or shoulders. Some of their heads were encased within large CRT televisions, their faces gleaming behind screens that distorted their features with rolling scanlines. Others wore more outlandish attire, like boombox breastplates or Power Glove gauntlets lined with rave lights. A few of them lugged what looked like large subwoofers under their arms, attached to their torsos via harnesses—they seemed to be aware of the precise moment the house's occupants became aware of them, because the haunting audio from *Operation Wandering Soul* started to howl from their speakers right on cue. *Wandering Soul*, a series of 'ghost' recordings by the U.S. Forces that made use of eerie sounds and altered voices, filled the surrounding woods with shrill screams and warped, drawn-out moans of supposedly fallen *Việt Cộng* soldiers. The invading force that encircled the house played these recordings in perfect synchronization from every side; thunderous reverb shook the house and rumbled in everyone's ears.

Marcy woke up screaming in terror, flailing her arms, sweeping glasses and plates off the table and sending them crashing to the floor. The children bawled and scrambled for places to hide, yelling over each other. Cassandra trembled furiously, leaning against the counter when her legs threatened to give out under her. Wilma sat in her spot with her hands over her ears, eyes clamped shut. Officer Jameson maintained his calm demeanour. And Jack…

Jack had had enough. He stormed out onto the deck with the revolver raised and fired a warning shot into the air. The

202

recordings stopped blasting on the cult's speakers, its final notes screeching into the far distance, eventually fading to nothing but a recent, disturbing memory. A startling silence took its place. The cult members made no further noise, nor did they move. Jack felt them all watching him, but he didn't get the impression that their reaction was out of fear. Instead, it seemed as though they were waiting for him to open a conversation.

So he did, shouting at the top of his lungs: "What the fuck do you want?!"

The black figures were statuesque for a moment longer, their TV screen faces grinning from ear to ear on poor-quality film.

A tree moved behind them; it didn't take Jack long to realize it wasn't a tree at all, but a man walking on four stilts installed to his knees and elbows with fully adjustable joint implants. This man was swathed completely in black electrical tape, but he carried no equipment with him except for a single microphone installed into the sagging elephant tube of his faux gas mask, on the end of which dangled a spherical speaker. His steady breathing hissed through the apparatus, broadcasted from every side of the property. His stilt-limbs elevated his body high enough to allow him easy passage over the heads of the other cult members without them having to move aside. Despite his unusual form, the man on stilts moved with the grace of a seasoned circus performer.

Jack had never seen anything like it in real life or on television. He couldn't look away. Every instinct screamed for him to run and hide from this approaching thing. Its uncanny, human-spider crawl brought it closer and closer in shuddering, jerky motions; Jack felt helpless to stop it. Its steady breathing quickened slightly, its hoarse rasping louder and louder. When it got close enough, its head hovering over the balcony railing, Jack thought it would never stop until it had impaled him on one of its stilts. He was about to run when it finally quit its advance. Overhead Christmas lights glinted dully off of its mask and cracked electrical tape bindings. He hadn't realized how tall it truly was until it loomed over him, its breathing apparatus level with the roof. Light glinted in the lenses of its mask as the thing looked down at Jack in a way

204

that seemed indescribable. It did not seem concerned by Jack or the gun in his trembling hands. Its breath plumed through filters hidden on both sides of its face mask, while it continued its steady rhythm of breathing.

"What are you?" Jack found himself asking it.

Its voice was metallic-sounding, as if delivered through a tin can. No distinction between male or female could be made. "We are evolved," it said.

As the cold winter chill enclosed around him, the gun's freezing steel pricked tenderly in Jack's fingers. "What do you want?"

"The woman."

"What woman?"

"The *woman*." The thing's neck extended forward, head dipping toward him, its breathing apparatus wobbling with the sudden movement. Jack recoiled. His backside thumped against the window. Everyone on the other side with the exception of Officer Jameson watched in silent terror. "She's growing stronger. We can all feel her. Bring her to us and we will allow you all to leave unharmed."

"I don't believe you. If that's all you wanted, you would've come forward hours ago. Why now?"

"Because we're bored now. And so, I come to you now with our collective demand."

"And if we refuse...?"

"You have until midnight to deliver her to us. Soon her revenants will come. No one will be saved from them. And once they've had their fill, we'll take those of you that have survived and whatever is left of you back with us."

Despite the cold, Jack's blood began to boil with rising anger. "You think you can torment us like this? Nobody else is dying tonight. Except you. I guarantee it."

"Don't make promises you can't keep," the thing warned him, though its tone suggested that it was amused by Jack's response. "*We* wouldn't kill you. That's what her revenants are for."

Without further prompt, the thing retracted its head and returned to its bizarre compatriots. Jack watched, stunned, as the mob shambled back into the darkness beyond the treeline. He watched them fade into black shapes, then shapeless blotches,

206

and then, long after they were no longer tangible from the shadows that concealed them, Jack remained where he stood in his petrified state.

"Jack." Cassandra snapped him out of it. She'd come out with his coat and draped it around his shoulders. "Come inside."

"I could have shot him. I could have ended things right there."

"Or you could've made it worse."

"You don't know that."

"Neither do you. Come inside, Jack. You're shaking like crazy."

Jack hadn't even noticed how cold he was until his wife had mentioned it. His fingers were stuck to the gun. He tried to pry them off the grip, but they were fused to it. Jack raised his hand and studied it closely, his heart beginning to race, questions swirling in his brain. His fingers had seemingly *merged* with the gun itself. "What the fuck...?" he gasped.

"Jack, come inside. Put the gun away."

"I... I *can't!*" With his left hand, Jack took hold of the revolver and pulled on it as hard as he could. The revolver's

207

muzzle remained pointed at the yard as he struggled to pry it loose with all of his strength. He felt his skin shift with the revolver's grip, felt piercing fire all the way to the bone. The revolver wouldn't come loose. "It's stuck! I can't..."

Cassandra found herself backing away from her husband as he grew more panicked. He hurled the gun around, unable to detach it. He smacked it on the brick window ledge, then the wall beside it, slicing his knuckles open, carving deep gashes between tendons; and when he still couldn't detach it, he started screaming. Hoarse, growling noises bellowed from his lungs as he slammed his gun-hand against the house's brick in a horrific display of desperation. His tantrum couldn't be tamed—Cassandra called his name several times in unheard attempts to calm him.

Finally, Jack pitched onto his knees, sending tremors through the deck. His coat slipped off his shoulders, landed in a heap. Clutching his gun-hand he twisted toward the trees. He shouted obscenities at their watchers and emptied the revolver into the random points of the treeline, hitting the railing once and then one of the lanterns

208

that lit the path around the pond. He wobbled back to his feet, ignoring Cassandra's continued attempts to get his attention while keeping a safe distance from his crazed tantrum. His words dissolved into guttural, animalistic snarls and howls. His voice shuddered as he sobbed. Fear and anger took hold.

He staggered toward the trees, fumbling awkwardly with the gun, eventually got the cylinder open. His free hand searched all of his pockets for more bullets. He pulled a few out, dropping more into the snow, and struggled to chamber them. His hands were shaking too violently for him to get more than four bullets chambered before his frustration got the better of him. He hurled the other bullets into the yard with a final, throaty howl that floundered into pitiable, shuddering sobs, and then collapsed in a heap just before the steps leading down to the yard.

A thought more chilling than the harsh winter air struck Cassandra. For a moment, she registered her husband's sobs as uncontrollable laughter. Even now that she was paying attention to it, she found it difficult to identify if he was crying in defeat or suffering a psychotic episode. Jack was never soft-spoken, nor was he always agreeable in his views or attitude, but he never made her feel threatened, not at his lowest.

For the first time in their marriage, Cassandra was too afraid to approach her husband. She'd never seen him lose his grip in five years of marriage. She turned to the faces in the window. "Somebody help me with him, *please!*"

Wilma was standing next to her before Cassandra noticed her absence from the audience around the kitchen table. She was calm, rubbing her own shoulders against the cold as she went to pick up Jack's coat. "Go to him, Cass," she said with hushed urgency. "Before he runs off into those woods."

Cassandra hesitated, then trudged through the ankle-deep snow to Jack. His sobs were quiet now. His shoulders jerked about as he cried hopelessly. She called his name, softly. "Jack?"

He didn't acknowledge her.

Wilma wrapped him in his coat and pressed herself against his back. "God, he's

210

ice-cold. Help me bring him in."

Cassandra took his unaltered arm while Wilma took his modified gun-hand, giving it a look of disbelieving horror. They lifted him up. His legs worked in feeble cooperation, half-dragging, as they carried him back inside.

"To the couch. Come on. Marcy, where are the kids?"

"Foyer," Marcy answered quietly. She was standing by the foyer, feeling helpless. The children were all huddled together there, bundled in their winter clothes and boots.

Cassandra took a cautionary glance at Officer Jameson as they passed him. Her mind went to the pistol tucked in her waistband. With Jack's arm over her shoulder and her current task of helping Wilma carry him to the couch, she couldn't stop him from taking her gun if he wanted to.

And he did. Jameson leaped out of his chair and hurtled straight at her. Cassandra twisted, falling against her husband and nearly shoving Wilma into the grandfather clock as she tried to evade him. Jameson's face twisted, distorted by his fast

211

movement, a blur of anger and concentration. Cassandra felt the gun leave her waistband. "Hey!"

He shoved her back with more power than she thought a human being could possess. It ripped the air from her lungs. The three of them fell in a heap on the floor, Jack and Cassandra piled on top of Wilma, who screamed out. Cassandra quickly rolled off and found herself on her hands and knees, staring up the barrel of Officer Jameson's pistol.

"Not. Another. Inch." Jameson's expression was indifferent again. His pistol hovered over the three family members, drifting back and forth, as if the gun itself was trying to decide which life to take first.

"You can't," Cassandra said, unable to hide the tremble in her voice. "You're a cop."

"One of those things is true. I am a cop." His pistol became adjacent with Wilma as she wriggled out from under Jack with great effort. When she saw the gun, her eyes widened. Her face pulled back, gentle features distending in horror.

He pulled the trigger.

212

Friday, December 15th, 2000 - Part X

The gun flashed. The sound of a sledgehammer pounding a cinderblock roared in everyone's ears. A shockwave rippled across the floor. Cassandra and Marcy screamed. Wilma's head snapped back against the wood flooring.

Cassandra's ears rang. Her body trembled. She was overcome with dread about what she would see if she turned her head. If she looked at Wilma. For a moment, the crazy thought that he hadn't done what she knew he'd done tried to give her false hope. Perhaps, so long as Cassandra didn't give in to her worst curiosity, if she didn't turn her head to visually confirm it, Wilma would still be alive.

She looked. She couldn't see Wilma's face so she leaned further over Jack. Tears poured down her cheeks as she registered the red blotches that speckled the nearby wall and the grandfather clock's glass case. The floor was covered in a dark pool shaped like a maple leaf, reflecting the

213

light from the kitchen in crimson shades. Cassandra saw tiny white fragments and fleshy clumps floating in it. A horrible buzzing behind her eyes paralyzed her as she stared at the look of terror frozen on the remaining half of Wilma's face, peering too deeply for her own good, into the one wide eye that stared into a void of death.

Cassandra choked on a scream, her mouth hanging open in shock. Her eyes withered as tears streamed out. Her mouth quivered. A scream finally came—loud, feral, and shrill.

Officer Jameson was so fixated on Cassandra doing something drastic that he hadn't noticed Marcy lifting a glass bowl of Caesar salad off the kitchen table until she'd smashed it against the back of his skull. Dressed lettuce and croutons as well as his own blood exploded over his shoulders and splashed to the floor. He pivoted awkwardly at a sideways angle. His face bounced off the table, knocking over his mug and shattering it on the floor, and then he plummeted after it. Officer Jameson didn't get back up. He didn't move an inch.

"The gun," Cassandra croaked,

214

choking on her tears.

Marcy wrenched the pistol from Jameson's hand and backed away from him with a blank look on her face. Her expression didn't change when she turned her head and saw Wilma's body sprawled on the floor, her legs half-hidden under Jack. "Are they…?"

Cassandra was staring at Officer Jameson.

"Cass."

Cassandra's glazed eyes flicked up, startled.

"Are they both…?"

"Just… just Mom."

Marcy sucked in a deep breath and closed her eyes, held her breath for a moment, then slowly exhaled. When she opened her eyes, she blinked furiously, but fresh tears still came. "Fuck," she said. "Fuck. Fuck. *Fuck*!"

The kids had been making slow progress across the kitchen, their curiosity luring them back to the living room. They could see Officer Jameson on the floor, but they couldn't see Wilma.

Cassandra heard them before she saw them and leaped into the kitchen. "No! Go

215

back to the foyer. Don't come in here."
Amidst a wave of protests, she shouted,
"GO! And don't move from there!"

Frightened, the kids returned to the
foyer and sat on the floor.

Cassandra rubbed her eyes. More
tears replaced the ones she'd just wiped
away. "God," she muttered to herself.
"Jesus, God, why?"

"You okay?" Marcy asked her.

"No, are you?"

Holding the pistol against her hip in
her left hand, Marcy dug her right hand into
her jeans pocket. Without breaking eye
contact with her sister-in-law, Marcy used
her right hand to put a cigarette in her
mouth, tuck the carton back in her pocket,
produce a match, scratch a flame on the
end, and light the cigarette. She no longer
caring that she was indoors. She inhaled its
toxins, blowing smoke between them.
"Want one?"

"I don't smoke."

"Good a time to start as any."

"No, thank you."

The two women watched each other
in silence, unsure of what to say or do. It
was Marcy who first broke eye contact,

216

glancing at each of the windows; first the ones in the living room, then the ones in the dining area, then the big one in the kitchen. She looked once again at Cassandra. "Take the keys to Mom's car and get the kids outta here."

"I'm not leaving Jack."

"Jack can take care of himself."

"He isn't even conscious."

"Don't be stubborn. We both know which one of us is the better parent."

"I never thought that. Not for a second."

"I know." Marcy flashed her with a wavering smile, attempting to mask her own pain. "But you're the better pick."

"Why, Marcy?"

"My mom's lying on the floor next to her own brains. My dad lost his mind. My brother just had a psychotic breakdown. Like father, like son, I guess. And my husband's charred corpse is freezing over in the driveway. Most importantly, I'm too drunk to drive five confused kids out of here. But *you* aren't."

"They need you."

"They need a parent."

"You're their parent."

217

"Look, I'm not delusional. While John helped Hannah with her math homework, I was watching TV. When John was keeping Bryan from running out into the street, I was drinking wine in the bathtub. Even now, the only useful thing I've done tonight is smash a salad bowl over a cop's head."

"No. No, Marcy."

"Just go."

"Marcy—"

"*GO!*" Marcy's shout startled Cassandra and the children. "Just get out! Leave!"

Something tapped the floor behind her. Marcy turned and looked down at the body of Officer Jameson, still sprawled face down on the floor, streaks of blood and salad dressing mingling in grotesque squiggles along the side of his head—but now one eye was open and staring up at her.

The grandfather clock struck the eleventh hour at a frighteningly high volume.

GONG

Lights flickered. The house shuddered violently. Dust rained down

218

from the ceiling. Marcy staggered away from the clock, covering her ears.

GONG

Cassandra screamed as the house seemed to jolt her against the island counter. Marcy sprang out of the living room, just as the third bell sounded.

GONG

Pictures burst from their frames on the walls. The living room chandelier smashed into the floor. Marcy dived across the kitchen floor, pure flight response to whatever was happening around her.

GONG

The clock's bells howled through the house. Some unseen force behind Marcy launched the dining room table and chairs off the floor and against the windows, flinging dishes that shattered against the walls and ceiling. One of the chairs spiraled across the living room over the couch and speared the Christmas tree.

GONG

Another explosion caused the buffet and hutch to erupt from its wall mount, spraying the living room with a deadly salvo of disintegrated china; antique splinters peppered the kitchen cupboards and living room floorboards, speckled the wallpaper like shotgun pellets.

GONG

Every lightbulb in the house seemed to pop all at once, dropping every room into a disorienting darkness lit only by the moon filtering through the windows.

GONG

The windows exploded inward, showering glass over every flat surface. The skylight rained down on the couch. The picture window disintegrated into a billion tiny particles, the snow-covered birdfeeders dangling from the soffit under the eavestrough burst apart.

The kids in the foyer screamed. Marcy and Cassandra both scrambled to protect them from glass and debris.

GONG

The kitchen table shot across the floor in pursuit of the two mothers. It made a thunderous noise as it skated across tile to cut off their escape.

"Marcy!" Cassandra took hold of Marcy's arm and yanked her into the foyer as the table closed the gap between them, banging into the doorframe.

GONG

220

Every kitchen cupboard flew open. Everything inside them filled the air like startled, misshapen birds. Cutlery shot out of drawers, a swarm of silver locusts buzzing angrily in the moonlit kitchen. Dishware spun about and smashed themselves against walls; some disappeared through the opening where the picture window once existed, clearing the deck and entering the trees.

GONG

Officer Jameson was floating in the midst of the storm of destroyed furniture, twisted cutlery, and flocks of twinkling glass. He dangled above the floor like a marionette suspended by invisible strings, his blood-covered body contorting strangely. An inhuman roar bellowed from deep within him, finally unleashed, and with it another violent shockwave surged through the house, stripping the walls bare and blasting the island counter into tiny pieces.

GONG

The final toll of the bell was punctuated by the grandfather clock exploding, blowing cogs, glass, and wood pieces across the living room. Portions of ceiling plaster crashed down. Jagged cracks coursed through the walls like bulging veins.

"This way!" Cassandra and Marcy led the children out into the garage. Hannah fell off the stairs and landed on the concrete floor with a whine. Alistair bolted straight for the front door.

"No, not that way!" Cassandra dragged him away from the door and practically carried him to Wilma's car.

"Shit," Marcy cried out, "the keys. Jesus, I don't have the keys—"

Marcy suddenly reeled backwards into the foyer, as if jerked hard by an invisible rope. She shrieked, reached out for help until her body slammed into the closet.

"Mom!" Bryan was paralyzed with fear, watching from the entrance as his screaming mother *flew* out of the closet and was swung about by an unseeable force, bouncing against the walls of the narrow foyer. Then a vacuum that defied all logic and physics sucked her back into the kitchen and dragged her helpless form through a sea of broken things that sliced and punctured her.

222

Bryan could still hear her screams, which triggered him to run in after her, only for Cassandra to grab hold of him and carry him flailing down the steps to the car. "Mom! Mom! Let go!"

"Get in the basement!" Cassandra snatched Hannah's wrist before she could act by her twin brother's example. Both children fought against her. "Please, we have to hide!"

"Let go of me! Mom! *Mooooomm*!"

Marcy wailed in agony and terror, limbs thrashing, as the invisible force plowed her body into the compartment under the sink, twisting her left ankle. She felt the force lift her again. She gripped the sink's pipe as tightly as she could as her body was lifted off the floor. "No-no-no-no-no-no-no—"

The pipe broke apart. She was then dragged out from beneath the sink, flung against the fridge. Her left arm crunched at a bad angle, snapping it in a terrible direction, inciting a shrill scream from her. She was thrown up against the ceiling, on which she spun a dizzying figure-eight before plummeting to the floor, sidewinding halfway to instead land heavily onto the countertop beside the sink. Her shin snapped in half, the foot attached to it slapping limply against the drain. The malevolent force dragged her from one end to the other. She collided with the toaster and the wall beside the living room entryway under the mounted landline, knocking the receiver off the hook. As she felt the force pull her off the counter, Marcy grappled with the telephone cord and held on. She hung suspended above the area where the island counter was reduced to a pile of wooden spikes and twisted metal amid clumps of smashed trinkets. Falling on it would leave her impaled on many pieces of structural wood that once held the island together. Marcy's tear-filled eyes stared down at the counter's pointed foundations. "Nuh-no-NO—"

The landline was uprooted from the wall. Now free, Marcy hurtled across the kitchen, banked sharply at a breakneck angle, her surroundings blurring past her. Her vision flashed white from the pain of her body smacking at full speed into the stone fireplace's overmantel. Her right kneecap split against the mantle. The force released her. Officer Jameson watched her

224

broken body tumble down the fireplace. Her face collided wetly with the hearth extension; her nose was violently inverted and her front teeth popped against the ledge. She rolled onto the floor, displacing a piece of fallen roof plaster. She sputtered blood through split lips, her face mangled and purple. Her nose was reduced to a black pit oozing blood, snot, and fragments of cartilage. Her head jerked wildly as she fought to breathe. She attempted to inhale through her new central cavity and choked instead. She coughed. Desperation gripped her. She breathed rapid, shuddering gasps through her bloody mouth. Her ears rang, sounding like the drawn-out peal of a bell. Her head and vision were trapped in a disorienting haze. She could faintly hear her children calling for her from the garage.

Officer Jameson's feet softly touched the floor. Bits of glass crunched under the soles of his shoes as his levitation slowly released his full body weight on solid ground. He approached Marcy's twisted body, watching her writhe pitiably. The TV had somehow survived the maelstrom he'd created with his psychic abilities. Ghostly flickering light emanated from the grainy

225

picture of a wheat field and black shore on its screen.

"I can't imagine how that feels," he said to her. He pressed his palm against the spot on his head where she'd smashed the salad bowl and looked at the blood and salad dressing that caked his hand in disgust. "This all could've been avoided. But noooo. You all had to listen to that crazy old man downstairs. I bet you don't even know why you were going along with it. *What* you were going along with."

He held up his hand, soaked in mostly blood diluted to a lighter pink thanks to the salad dressing. The vinegar stung his wounds, making him wince. "You see this? This is fluid of a physical body. This is what spills out of a person who has not ascended. I feel *pain*. Fuck, this hurts. I know, I'm preaching to the choir. I bet you know what pain feels like, huh? Your flesh limits you."

Marcy gurgled and spat blood and more teeth. Her swollen eyes rolled in a daze.

Officer Jameson took another step, crushing a slab of plaster to chalk dust under his feet. "That bitch, the one you've

226

all been harboring, promised us a greater existence, a *higher* existence, ascension beyond the limitations of our flesh. The new millennium was supposed to bring the next stage of evolution for us all! But *she* took that from us! *Stole* it from us! Abused it, *perverted* it, let her dipshit son fuck around with his neighbours' kids and wives, his mom, his sister—while we had to scorch the earth looking for what she took from us all those years ago. Does that sound fair to you? To be robbed of your right to join the noise, to even *see* it, just so some punk creep can get his dick wet with vegetative organ packets?"

Somehow she managed to roll onto her side with a strained groan. Her right arm was still intact. She used it to drag herself along the floor to the TV.

Officer Jameson gaped at her efforts. "Amazing! You're more resilient than any of us would've expected. Maybe all that alcohol dulled the pain." He chuckled quietly as he watched her slow progress toward the TV. Every movement elicited another miserable groan from her. "Where do you think you're going?"

A growling moan gurgled from her

227

throat as she struggled to crawl further. Her left eye had been blackened, swollen shut. Her right eye was less damaged, fixed on the TV screen, focused on the figure walking through the field. John, or someone who looked like John, bearing his winning smile and flowing locks of curly hair.

"Dust," he said as he shambled closer.

Marcy flopped forward with her right arm stretched out. She realized it wasn't John. She could feel John nearby, but whoever she was looking at wasn't him.

She blacked out.

Officer Jameson wasn't gloating anymore, anyway. His face blanched when he saw the screen. He reached toward the shambles that covered the kitchen floor. His Beretta appeared in his hand. He turned it on the TV and fired a shot into the set.

The screen didn't go black with a hole in it. The bullet didn't blast through the back of the television set. Instead, the bullet passed through the screen into the picture, whizzed across the field into the eye of the charred revenant that had been thawing in this milder weather for hours.

228

The revenant's head snapped back. A chunk of its rotting cranium burst through its scalp, spilling black, congealed liquid onto its back. The cranium piece was stuck to its torn scalp by clumps of matted hair, and as the revenant resumed its shambling, the back of its head flapped loosely between its shoulder blades.

"Jesus—"

"Dust," it said.

Officer Jameson staggered back. He heard wood creak down the hall and jerked his gun in that direction and fired into the darkness. The gun flashed, illuminating the corridor, revealing John's elongated revenant standing there on all four stilt-like limbs, stooped beneath a ceiling that was far too low for his towering, inhuman height, eyes glazed white, grinning jaw stretched grotesquely from his pitted nose to his groin, needle-shaped teeth as long and narrow as swamp reeds.

Jameson let out a primal shriek. Fired another round into the corridor and then ran full-tilt across the kitchen, clearing a path through the debris with his psychic powers.

He bounded through the foyer, leaped off the stairs, fell on his side, got back up, and darted alongside Wilma's car to the basement door. He grabbed hold of the doorknob. Locked. He stepped back and swung his arm out. The door was torn to splinters by a mere thought, the window in it blowing glass. He peeked down the stairs into the basement. The ceiling lights were off. Incandescent, flickering blue light illuminated the walls. Officer Jameson could see black stains on the floor at the foot of the stairs.

Slowly, gripping his gun, he descended the stairs. Each step creaked in protest against his weight, but each step held. Jameson made quick work of his descent, taking in his bearings. The bank of TVs stacked against the wall under the stairs cast dark, distorted shadows along the far wall. The entire room was cluttered, but seemingly devoid of human life. The shelves, desks, pool table, and stacks of boxes would provide plenty of potential hiding places. With his back to the wall, Officer Jameson scanned the basement for signs of life, his gun sights perfectly mirroring where his trained eyes went.

Something slithered in a glass tank on the desk. A woman's husky, seductive

230

voice said, "Hello, Henry."

Jameson gasped and fired at the head rising out of the tank. The head sporting blonde, shoulder-length hair, mounted on a slender neck, on two shoulders from which two arms had sprouted. The arms were crossed over the tank's ledge, supporting the woman as she leaned over it, her full, naked breasts pressed enticingly against the glass. Her hypnotic eyes, even in the dim glow of the televisions, paralyzed him, frightened him, ensnared him just as they had once before.

She took the bullet directly into her forehead. Her expression didn't change. The hole in her head closed up behind the bullet. She opened her mouth; the mushroomed bullet rolled off her tongue and hit the floor with a solid clattering. She chuckled. "I've tasted better."

Dan Snr appeared at the top of the stairs and aimed his index finger at him in the imitation of a gun, and shouted a playful "Bah-*BANG*!"

Shocked, Officer Jameson looked up at him. The two men stared at each other for a beat. Jameson's fearful eyes contrasted against Dan Snr's manic grin.

231

Jameson brought up his pistol.

Dan Snr fired his shotgun from the hip.

*

The shot echoed through the house, startling Marcy from unconsciousness. Stunned, numb, she looked up at the ceiling, her vision clouded by blood trickling down her forehead. She coughed. John looked down at her, his proportions normal and strikingly warm. As if he'd never died. As if he'd never burned. An angel? Was she dead or dying? She didn't care. She couldn't feel pain anymore. She reached for him, her love for him swelling like the dozens of bruises inflicted upon her body, blood bubbling from her split lips as she tried to smile.

"My handsome man."

John lifted her gently off the floor and cradled her in his arms. "My love. It'll all be over soon."

"The kids?" She didn't question how she could speak normally now.

"They're okay. They're sleeping upstairs. I only managed to get a few chapters into *Princess Bride* before they dozed off."

232

"Naturally." She shared a passionate kiss with her husband. It was *him*. *His* warm embrace. *His* muscular arms. *His* lips. It was what she chose to see in her final moments.

The revenant closed its jaws on her head. Its needle-teeth skewered her skull in a dozen places, cracking it wide open and spilling its contents into the revenant's gullet.

Cameron Morgan's revenant crawled through the television screen, static crackling around it as it wormed its way through. "Dust," it said, and together they devoured Marcy Carmichael.

Friday, December 15th, 2000 - Part XI

One hour earlier.

Dan Snr busied himself with reading a written witness testimony of the events at the roadside motel glimpsed in some of the tapes. Occasionally he glanced at the organic pustules in the mass of flesh growing out of the videotape within the confines of the fish tank. After he checked the videotape organism's progress, he always looked at the bank of surveillance feeds along the far wall. So far, the cult members were behaving themselves. Their most heinous act, so far, was the continuous and abortive attempt at breaking the light above the driveway with snowballs.

When he noticed the formation of an eyeball, he lost complete interest in the document, instead focusing his full attention on this new progress. The eyeball quivered beneath a thin, milky film, embedded in the center of a much larger mass of gnarly, pulsating flesh. The videotape carapace had further expanded and appeared to be degrading, melting or

234

fusing with the organic material expanding out of it.

Dan Snr hovered over the eye. The eye seemed to be fixed on him. He moved to a different position on the other side of the desk. The eye followed. Dan Snr, excited now, went around again, his back now facing the TVs. The eye followed. Dan Snr proceeded with a third test: he ducked under the desk, crawled on his hands and knees to the other side, and slowly, quietly raised himself back up, hunched forward, peeking over a pile of documents at it. The eye, having been looking toward the wall at the foot of the stairs, suddenly locked onto him. It gave his old heart a small start.

"God," he mumbled in astonishment. He searched the desk's drawers for a penlight, found one in the third drawer down, and shined it delicately into the eye. The pupil dilated in response. "Amazing! Barely a face, yet you're already displaying reflexes and cognitive behaviour as if fully formed..."

He put on a fresh pot of coffee in the corner and returned from the percolator with a fresh mug, black, no cream, no sugar; WORLD'S GREATEST DETECTIVE etched on the mug in bold font. He sat on his stool and silently waged a staring contest with the eye, watching the growth around it continue to build new tissue over existing tissue. Total cellular reconstruction was happening before his eyes. He was so spellbound by it that when the thought crossed his mind to get it all on video, he cursed himself for his forgetfulness.

He scrambled, grabbing the video camera, mounting it on a tripod, and situating it against the wall by the work bench, aiming its lens straight at the fish tank. He made sure a blank tape had been inserted. Then he ran it.

Sitting on his stool, he watched the specimen in the tank. His only partial distraction was his cup of coffee. It seemed only minutes had flashed by before a woman's face formed in the clay-like flesh; a narrow, pointed nose, a second eye, a broad forehead, and a delicate mouth that rasped its first breath, as if she'd just come up from the deep end of a swimming pool for air.

"Hello," he said, awkwardly. "Donna

236

Anderson, I presume?"

The face stared at him. Opened its mouth. A deep rasp gurgled out of lips that tried to form words. Its vocal chords hadn't grown in, yet. The sound made Dan Snr's flesh crawl, but despite his aversion to the sight and sound of this woman-thing growing inside the tank, he didn't look away from her steely gaze, even as her mouth continued to make those awful sounds. The plastic carapace of the videocassette strained to contain her as she continued to grow. Her head appeared to be stretching as it squeezed through the narrow opening in the videotape. In five minutes, her ears had pulled through. Her head was smooth and bald at first; white-blond strands of hair began to worm out of her scalp as she further materialized.

Dan Snr stood up from his stool. He was far too excited to sit still. He paced the room, eyes fixed on her, drinking from his mug until it was empty, refilling it, and then draining it in less than ten minutes. Just finding something to do to pass the time. He was no longer paying attention to the surveillance feeds.

She'd managed to wriggle the rest of

237

her jawline out of the tape. Her eyes rolled upwards as an obscene moan scraped from her partially formed throat. More of her head wriggled out. The carapace splintered with a loud snap. She grunted in response. Her breathing quickened.

Dan Snr found himself standing over the tank, watching her with intense curiosity. "Can you understand me?"

"Yes," she gasped.

Startled by her vocal response, Dan Snr took a step back, only to approach the tank again with newfound fascination. "You can finally speak."

"Yes."

Dan Snr didn't want to tiptoe around the questions he'd been brewing in his mind since he first delved into the documents and tapes the police had provided him. "How did this happen?"

"That is… a loaded question." She seemed to be short of breath. Her lungs hadn't fully formed yet.

"We'll put a pin in that, for now." Noticing his coffee mug was empty again, Dan Snr set it down on the desk. "What world are you from?"

"*Earth*, moron."

238

Frowning, Dan Snr said, "Nice to see I've brought more sarcasm into this household. Fine." He sat on the stool, propped his elbows on his raised knees, and made a tent with his fingers. "I'll elaborate: *where* have you been recently?"

"The Noise."

"'The Noise'?"

"White... Noise." Before Dan Snr could ask, she continued, "It is... all-encompassing. Home for things... we never dreamed of."

"What things?"

"*Things.*"

"That's not very helpful."

"Let's change the subject."

"But—"

She fixed him with a cold, paralyzing glare. "Okay," he said, uneasily. "We'll put a pin in that, too."

The haunting moans and shrieking wails of *Operation Wandering Soul* filled the house. The rafters reverberated from the deep, rumbling bass of the cult's surround-sound attack. Dan Snr glanced at the bank of televisions and saw *them* emerging from the shadows, abstract shapes shambling through knee-deep snow. They

239

were starkly black shapes clashing with the perfect blue-white terrain they crossed. Not quite human anymore, carrying themselves like exhausted circus performers. They resembled a herd of assorted animals, apes or orangutans that had fused metal, electrical equipment, and latex to themselves. They didn't move like people.

Somehow, Donna Anderson seemed to know what Dan Snr was looking at. "Worshippers of the Noise."

"What exactly do they want?"

"The Noise."

"How do we get rid of them?"

"You can't. Not without the power of the Thoughtographers."

"Thoughtographers? What are they?"

"Worshippers of the Noise."

Dan Snr took a moment to think. So far his questions had led him into dead ends or full circles. He grunted in frustration, picked up his shotgun and inspected it.

"What are you doing?"

"Preparing myself against these 'Thoughtographers' you hold in such high regard."

"You cannot kill a Thoughtographer. Not that easily."

240

"Are you saying they're invincible?"

"Nothing is invincible."

"*What*, then? How do they have these powers?"

"Inheritance."

"From *what*?" Dan Snr shouted. "Bloodlines? Medical procedures?" As his frustration grew, his tone became derisive. "For Christ's sakes, were they struck by lightning in a goddamn laboratory? Or maybe the gods gifted them with these abilities."

Donna Anderson's head fell back against the glass as her neck sprouted from the tape like a thick weed, exposing her throat, which undulated as she swallowed. She sucked in air and rasped, "The Noise. They sought it out. It came. Those who didn't lose their minds... or their lives... those who weren't rejected became... more. Like I did. I became more. I was... just a woman. I followed the teachings. I liberated myself... from my moral upbringing... my physical aversions to... all things. I became... *more*. Spiritually. Then physically. Sexually. Psychologically. I ascended. Liberated from my flesh. My mind swelled. My

241

body... merely a tool, a vessel... for breeding, for appearances... among those who remain blissfully unaware. Unaware of their true potential. The Noise can only be found, and heard... through the analog medium."

Dan Snr absorbed this, and noticed that *Wandering Soul*'s broadcast had ended abruptly after the muffled thump of a gunshot. He looked to the surveillance feeds again and saw Jack standing on the deck, face-to-face with a spider-like man. He couldn't hear their conversation. "Is that why they're after you? Because you left the cult? 'You can check out any time you like, but you can never leave'?"

"No. They aren't after me because I left. They're after me because I took the Noise."

"Where did you take it?"

"I hid it."

"Where did you hide it?"

"My poor boy. The Noise corrupted him, as it had corrupted us all. My daughter, my darling little girl... volunteered to be its concubine. Her body was so smooth. So perfectly soft. Her flesh was so pleasurable. We severed her ties to

242

her body far too prematurely. Not even the Noise can taste her now."

Dan Snr shuddered. He was speechless. He stiffened when he realized she wasn't finished yet. "I was not born this way. The Noise took me in. Changed me. Melted into me. Filled me."

An intrusive thought flashed through Dan Snr's mind; of Donna Anderson, whole again, floating in a vast space, her clothes disintegrating, exposing her perfect figure to him. Dan Snr blinked, furrowing his brow with confusion.

"We became one," she said. The videocassette was pulled apart by her right shoulder. Translucent fluid glistened as it oozed down her partially exposed collarbones. "I am the noise in your televisions; I am the void that stares back at you through your screen. Behind each screen, a window."

The intrusive thought persisted. She was staring at him in his mind, lying on her back, spreading her legs, beckoning him, welcoming him. He found himself panting; the confines of his pants suddenly restricted him…

"Behind each window, a door.

243

Behind each door, the Noise. Inheritance. I am the images on your screen. Gaze into me. Drink me in. Taste me. I shall bear the children of your thoughts."

Dan Snr floated in the void with her. They embraced. She pulled him in, gasping as he entered her. A manic surge of sexual energy took him like never before; he snatched her thighs and viciously thrust himself into her, watching her breasts roll and bounce from his vigorous movements. Her youthful body was his to ravage. "Your memories," she whispered, transforming herself, appearing as Wilma in her prime, her face smooth, her breasts full, her body firm and soft. "Your fantasies." Cassandra appeared under him, naked and exposed, vulnerable, screaming with pleasure as he drove himself inside her—

"Stop it! *NO!*" Dan Snr hurled himself out of the void. He crashed into the office chair and toppled over with it to the floor. He didn't feel any pain. His eyes darted around the room fearfully. The basement spun around him. His skull buzzed painfully, his eyes felt like they'd been stabbed with needles. His skin was clammy, drenched in sweat. He groaned,

244

falling on his side, waiting for the room to stop spinning.

A loud crack thumped through the ceiling. At first, Dan Snr thought he'd knocked something over, but a second and then a third consecutive crack made him realize he was hearing the reports of more gunshots. He crawled toward the wall of televisions and saw Wilma and Cassandra rushing out across the deck toward something off screen. He couldn't see Jack.

"They're here," Donna said.

Dan Snr pushed himself up onto his knees, turned, and looked at her. Her head was still on its left ear, her eyes boring into him through the fish tank's murky glass walls. Her head was attached to a pulpy mass of undulating flesh and black plastic from which three tiny digits were protruding just under her collarbones. "Who?" he asked. "*Who?*"

Donna giggled, wiggling her exposed digits teasingly.

Dan Snr gaped at her in disbelief, and was about to voice his disgust at her when another gunshot barked, this one louder than before. His eyes searched the bank of screens, but he didn't have any cameras

245

mounted inside the house. He heard Cassandra scream. His blood curdled. His limbs wobbled like jelly. He knew. Somehow, he knew why she screamed. "The cop. Jesus, *the cop!*" He grabbed the shotgun off the table and started up the stairs. "Stupid—I was so stupid! Wilma! Jack!" He slipped on the third step, lost his footing, and tumbled back down to the floor, inciting a shrill laugh from Donna Anderson. He couldn't feel any pain—his blood was pumping too quickly—he felt only desperation and rage. "Shut up!" he growled at her. "Bringing you through was a mistake."

"Perhaps, for you—but I'm grateful to you all the same." Four digits extended further from each side of her, like a spider's legs, thin and elongated human fingers. She looked like the result of some sick-minded sculptor; an arthropod made from human body parts. Her neck stretched out to accommodate her finger-legs. Her head swayed unsteadily as her digits lifted her off the floor of the tank, revealing a red bulbous organ loosely packaged in a thin, translucent pink film extending out of the videocassette beneath her, caged behind

246

three half-finished ribs. Dan Snr could hear her heart beating behind the translucent layer, causing the shapeless crimson mass within it to surge and swell against its calcium confines. Her other organs gurgled and sucked as they crawled out of the videocassette around the blood vessels connected to her heart, eliciting pleasurable moans from her. Her head lolled from side to side, her eyes rolling back as she cried out from sensations Dan Snr couldn't even begin to comprehend; she trembled, grunting as her innards crowded the tank, slapping wetly against the glass, smearing it with her blood and other fluids. Every one of her internal organs wriggled in a synchronized rhythm, but with distinctive personalities of their own. Her head rose up out of the tank, wobbling precariously on an oscillating bulk of slithering gore, her mouth open in an ecstatic grin. She ran her tongue around her moist lips as her flesh melted and spilled over her ribcage, forming her breasts and pink, hard nipples.

Dan Snr staggered away from her, repulsed, aroused, and confusingly revolted by his own arousal from her overtly sexual rejuvenation.

Her hands sprouted from shoulders that had just taken form, and then Dan Snr watched with mounting horror and breathless astonishment as her shoulders extended into two lithe stalks that bent with newly formed joints in the middle of them. Her palms touched the rim of the tank, her fingernails scraping the outer side of the glass.

Her eyes opened wide and she cried out in frenzied delight, the tendons popping in her neck, the glass cracking against her rigid fingers. Her orgasmic screams overlapped with Officer Jameson's howling upstairs. The lights fluttered. The shelves rattled. The TV screens flickered sporadically; the television mounted on the top left corner crashed to the floor. Dust and little pieces of debris rained down on Dan Snr, who pressed himself against the wall to avoid a possible collapse. A deep roar filled his ears, broken by the tolls of the grandfather clock, as what he could only assume was a violent maelstrom tore through everything built above the ceiling rafters.

The timing was too perfect. Dan Snr pointed his shotgun at Donna, squinting

248

against the persistent downpour of sawdust, insulation fluff, and pecks of old paint. "Stop this! Stop it!" He couldn't bring himself to shoot. "I'll shoot, damn you!" He couldn't close his finger on the trigger. Was it fear? Was it due to some perverse attraction to her beauty? Was it stubbornness? Had he truly gone too far to destroy her now? All he knew was that he could bring himself to touch the trigger and tease the notion of destroying her without going through with it.

The deafening racket ended almost as quickly as it began. The house stopped shaking. Donna's screams faded into heavy gasps, a satisfied look on her face. Chest heaving, skin glistening pink with sweat and blood, Donna Anderson gazed coyly at Dan Snr, her piercing eyes watching him between curtains of white-blond hair, tinged red. She was fully formed down to her waist, now. To Dan Snr, she appeared to be a normal woman sitting in a tank that was overflowing with blood and innards.

"It's been a while," she sighed. "If I had something to eat, this would go by much more faster."

Dan Snr's mouth worked, but no

sound came out. He was too overtaken by his own terror to do anything except sit against the wall and point his erect penis and loaded shotgun at the naked woman situated on his desk.

He heard the women and children screaming upstairs. He heard banging carry through the house. Bloodcurdling shrieks seemed to follow the sounds of impact through the foyer into the kitchen.

Dan Snr forced himself to get a grip. He rolled clumsily onto his feet and hurried over to the video camera he'd set up earlier. He ejected the tape, ignoring Donna Anderson's mocking questions and witty jabs. Shoved it and the tape he'd shown Jack into an empty padded mailing envelope side by side, with the 'TO WHOM IT MAY CONCERN' envelope slid in beside them. He sealed it with tape and scribbled an Upper Michigan address across it with black permanent marker.

He tucked the package under his arm and scuttled up the stairs with the shotgun at his side. Hannah and Brian were crying for their mother in the garage. He heard Cassandra yell at them to stay with her on the other side of the door. He reached the

250

top, opened the door and staggered into the garage. The children flocked him, sobbing and wide-eyed. Cassandra followed close behind them, dragging Brian with her. Her face was white, her eyes fearful, glittering with tears that hadn't yet rolled down her face.

"What's happening?" he asked her.

Marcy's shrill screams cut through the walls. Something smashed.

Cassandra saw the shotgun and nearly reached for it, but Dan Snr shoved the package into her hand, said, "Keep it safe!" and dashed by her and the child she was restraining. He reached the stairs and ran up into the foyer, bracing the shotgun against his shoulder. He caught a glimpse of Marcy flying out of the kitchen. He heard her collide with the fireplace but didn't see it. He knew just from the wet packing sound. He reached the kitchen entrance, partially blocked by the table, and gaped in disbelief at the destruction left in Officer Jameson's wake.

Then he saw her.

And froze.

His baby had been twisted and smashed into an unrecognizable, twitching

251

pulp splayed out in front of the hearth extension. His mouth hung open uselessly. The shotgun nearly slipped from slackening fingers. His heart pounded in his chest, each beat a painful twist of a knife. His little girl.

A shadow stepped into his line of sight. Just his shoulder, arm, part of his leg—the rest was hidden behind the wall. Dan Snr wasn't sure if his shotgun would penetrate the wall with enough force to stop the man behind it. His hands were quivering too much. Something in him made him afraid to interrupt whatever the man was saying to Marcy.

Marcy, who was lying on pieces of the ceiling as well as a scattering of her own teeth, her broken bones stretching under skin in odd ways, jutting, like tent poles raising fleshy canopies, was still alive. Dan Snr knew this because of the sounds she was making. Those horrible bubbling groans broken by violent coughing fits.

Dan Snr squeezed around the kitchen table, shotgun aimed at the ceiling with his finger on the guard. It was nearly impossible to step anywhere without

252

making noise, but it seemed as though Officer Jameson was too preoccupied with the sound of his own voice to notice. He opted to quietly shift things aside with his foot to keep from crunching them. He only made it a few inches before deciding that he couldn't get any closer without making too much noise. The kitchen was absolutely destroyed; littered, piled high with debris and utensils. Dan Snr eased himself back into the doorway, shaking furiously and cursing himself for his own cowardice. His eyes welled up with tears. He gritted his teeth, straining against his heartbreak, sucking in air, holding it, blowing it out.

Was it cowardice? It felt like it. Dan Snr was on the verge of running away, back into the basement where it was safe.

For reasons Dan Snr couldn't comprehend, Officer Jameson shrieked. It sent Dan Snr into his own panic. As Jameson fired his gun at whatever he saw, Dan Snr rushed back into the foyer, tripped over a pair of boots. Jameson's manic shouting chased him. Dan Snr threw himself into the closet, seeking safety in the crowd of hanging coats and umbrellas. A second later, Officer Jameson screamed by him. Dan Snr would have dropped the gun if he wasn't momentarily paralyzed with the fear of being discovered, but he quickly realized Jameson had entered the garage and was making his way toward the basement. He flinched as a loud crash resonated through the house. The tinkling of shattered glass spraying the concrete floor and the hollow clunking of wood peppering the walls followed. He heard Jameson's feet pounding down the stairs.

Dan Snr carried the shotgun into the garage and descended the stairs to the cold, smooth floor. He checked around the other side of Wilma's car and saw Cassandra huddled together with the other children, covered in wood chips and little glass particles. He put his finger to his lips and shushed them.

A gunshot thundered from below. Hannah whimpered. The rest of the children managed to keep quiet, tears streaming down their little faces as they huddled close to Cassandra.

Dan Snr heard Donna saying something to Jameson, but couldn't make out what it was. He heard something clatter on the floor as he reached the doorway.

254

He saw Officer Jameson standing aimlessly at the bottom of the stairs. The lights in the garage's rafters cast Dan Snr's shadow over him, alerting the frightened cop to the old man's presence. The look of horror on Jameson's face brought a surge of cruel satisfaction through Dan Snr, who smiled and used his free hand to point his index finger at him in the imitation of a gun. "Bah-*BANG*!"

Officer Jameson, startled, was frozen in place. He didn't move. Didn't speak. Didn't blink. He just stared, dumbfounded.

Then he raised his pistol, the moment Dan Snr was waiting for; the first twitch of Officer Jameson's tendons was all it took for Dan Snr to bring up the shotgun and blast him from the hip. The explosion was deafening in the narrow stairway, amplified by their tight, wooden confines.

Officer Jameson shouted when the shot ripped through his side, twirled with its momentum, scurried deeper into the basement where it was darkest, leaving bright red splotches from his wounds on the floor, and a trail of smears for Dan Snr to follow.

Saturday, December 16th, 2000 - Part I

A tittering sound echoed in the swirls of darkness clouding his mind. He swam back, sluggishly, to the murky shallows of consciousness. He opened his eyes and felt nothing but cold. Vision was fuzzy, taking too long to focus. His head throbbed with a burning sensation from the scalp. His nerves were all numb. He tried moving his fingers. He could feel the tingling sensation of movement, but he couldn't feel his fingertips rubbing together on one of his hands. His other hand was weighted down and immoveable. He stirred, found himself buried in darkness. He felt like he was trapped in the vacuum of space, shrinking into its cosmic void to be consumed and forgotten. There was nothing out here. No light, no life, no sound other than a thrumming low-frequency hum that sent sickly tremors through his body. He screamed but couldn't hear it; either his vocals were muted or he'd gone deaf to everything but that sickening noise and the slow rising and falling of its...

256

...Breathing...

The endless, empty space seemed to condense around him as it breathed, rising and falling, as he spun and spun and spun into deeper blackness...

The swirling darkness had dragged him back from the murky shallows into its depths that light couldn't penetrate.

An eye stared back at him. Disembodied, it floated freely in the blackness, spiraling, exacerbating his queasiness. That tittering sound again, like it was mocking his helplessness. It spun faster until it was a white ring.

He saw half of his mother's face staring back at him, her remaining eye swinging back and forth like a ball on Newton's cradle. The left half of her face slid up and down her scattered brains and severed nerves which blurred together in a long, crimson smear.

Mom's dead, he realized. *Oh God Mom's dead.*

Jack turned over and vomited on the floor. Wood flooring. He could feel it. He could *see* it. The void had a floor. His eyes searched this way and that, finding details he hadn't noticed before—debris scattered all around him, an overturned couch, walls with holes and fissures torn into them, a television set through which a soft breeze whistled; a front door that had been blown open.

A black figure was framed in the doorway against a backdrop of bluish white snow. The only detail Jack could make out was a pair of stark white circles where the figure's eyes must have been. Heavy boots crunched melting snow into the wood flooring as he approached. Something big and apparently heavy was strapped to the figure's back. He cradled something long and narrow. A gun? It sparked. A bright red tongue lashed out of the end. Jack's heart pounded as he realized—it was a flamethrower. The fire cast a grotesque sheen on the figure's homemade armour of flexible ductwork, clear nylon, and electrical tape. He wore a full-face diving mask, skewed slightly by a pair of large headphones clamped over his bald head. Jack could hear his breathing hiss through the apparatus.

The intruder ignored Jack for the time being, instead focusing on something Jack couldn't see from beneath the pile of ceiling debris that covered him.

Something tittered. He heard John tell the man to fuck off.

"Dust," said another stranger that Jack couldn't see.

The flamethrower roared as it filled the room with evening sunlight. Jack turned away, blinded by the light and surprised by the scorching heat on his face.

Something screeched worse than nails running down a blackboard. Jack clamped his hands over his ears, watching with eyes bulging in terror as the figure sprayed a monstrosity he couldn't see until the entire living room burned. The Christmas tree bellowed its last as it shriveled to death in the inferno. The screeching was from *something else*; the creature's shrieks deepened to distorted, guttural howls. A man-sized creature, engulfed in a blanket of fire, dived through the screen of the television set and disappeared, much to Jack's astonishment. He couldn't comprehend what he just saw at first.

Something big hurtled past the TV set, crashed into the Christmas tree and tackled it through the window into the front yard.

The man with the flamethrower swore as he charged back out the front door and assaulted the larger creature with another blast from his flamethrower, eliciting another howling screech. The dying screams of a broken air raid siren, garbled by decay, echoed into the night.

Jack scrambled out from under his pile of debris. He fell on his knees, disoriented. Both entries to the kitchen were blocked off by the upturned table and the uprooted dishwasher. Jack's hand burned as the revolver it was fused to grew hotter by the second. He tried to pry his fingers from it, but his skin seemed to have been completely melted into the grip somehow. He could feel the pearl handle touching the bones in his palm and fingers.

He peered down the corridor, untouched by fire, but the shadows within it were occupied by the charred, upright corpse of Deb, who tittered again as she lumbered in from the master bedroom. The inferno danced in her wide, empty eyes and blackened teeth showing through a Glasgow smile. Her hair was gone, her frame much thinner now that most of her had previously burned off in the driveway, and she was mostly obscured in the dark shadows of the hall. The flames distorted what little of her Jack could see, but there was no mistaking her for anyone else.

Her tittering followed Jack into the foyer, toward the front door. The man with the flamethrower saw him from the doorstep and turned his weapon in his direction. The thought of dying the same way Deb had kicked Jack's reflexes into high gear. The flamethrower filled his vision with blinding orange. Jack dived over the couch and tumbled to the floor. The foyer was transformed into a wall of flame that cascaded up the high walls and roiled in the ceiling's exposed studs, igniting the insulation.

Deb danced in the foyer, cheering maniacally as she twirled like an inexperienced ballerina.

Jack had no choice. He crawled to the TV and looked through it at the field of tall grass, patches of which had been ignited by the burning man who came before him. He chanced it. Pulled himself through the screen and pitched forward. Soft earth caught him. He rolled out of the burning grass, sprang to his feet, tumbled

261

awkwardly, leaped back up, and zigzagged until he was out of the burning grass. He patted himself down and checked for burns on his skin, and frayed edges of clothing that might still be alight. He was singed, hot, still feeling dizzy, but he wasn't going to die of immolation, and he wasn't in his parents' house anymore.

Jack took in his surroundings, stunned by the sudden change of climate and scenery. It was pleasantly warm here; the air smelled of saltwater in a calming breeze, tinged with acrid smoke. He turned to his right and saw more undulating fields of tall grass. To his left, he saw a smouldering figure flailing his arms as he blazed a trail in the grass in a desperate rush for the shoreline. Jack looked beyond the figure, at the sparkling, turquoise water the figure was trying to reach, as it reflected sunlight hidden above gunmetal grey clouds with impossible brightness. The black figure slowed, crumpled, shrank into a falling curtain of black smoke, never to reach the foamy waves of the ocean. The breeze carried his final word to Jack's ears in the form of a whisper: "Maureen."

Jack shuddered as he realized who—

262

or what—that thing used to be.

There was nothing out here but grass and water. He felt weightless. Uneasiness crept up from his core as he took another look around. He turned, contemplating a suicidal return to the house, imagining a daring escape through the flames and a bold rescue of his own family, when he saw something that demanded his attention far more than the little square portal hanging suspended in the air.

About fifty yards behind the portal was total, impregnable blackness. It stretched across the horizon, slicing through the ocean on one side and the grass fields on the other. It divided the sky itself, possibly reaching space. If there was an end to the world, it had to be here. The wall had no shadow. It appeared simultaneously as a solid wall and an empty space.

Jack felt drawn to it. He crossed the field. He passed the portal, itself a two-dimensional slice in the air that he could see around. He closed the gap between himself and the massive black wall. He had to know what it was. The nearer he approached, the louder its distorted hum

263

became. He could feel his bones vibrating from its frequency. It tickled his ears. All the tiny components in his gun-hand rattled.

It was only when he stood three feet away from it that he could truly appreciate its vastness. He craned his neck and looked straight up. The wall seemingly had no end in any direction, not even up. It reached past the clouds, maybe even beyond the sun. The wall had no apparent texture. Light had no effect on it. It appeared to Jack that this wall wasn't a structure made by people. No building materials could be seen from it. No flaws. Just a perfect, flat, smooth surface. It was the blackest black he'd ever looked at.

He raised his gun-hand and fired a round into the wall. The muzzle flash was not reflected on the wall. The bullet didn't embed itself into the wall, or bounce off in fragments—it completely vanished without leaving a mark. Jack silently concluded that it was neither a solid nor a liquid; it was a void.

Jack searched the grass for a stick. When he found one about fifteen inches in length, he returned to the wall, hesitated, and then prodded the wall gently with the stick. He felt zero resistance. The stick entered the wall and emerged unscathed. Jack tried again, thrusting the whole stick into the wall until the alien material nearly touched his hand. He was careful not to let it touch him. He pulled the stick out and studied it. The stick hadn't been altered in any way. He tapped it against a nearby rock. It still sounded like a stick. He tapped his gun-hand with it. It felt just like any old stick without as much as a difference in temperature.

Confounded, Jack stared at the wall. It reminded him of a black hole. But the gravitational density of a black hole would have spaghettified him long before he'd get the chance to poke it with a stick.

His curiosity persisted. He raised his gun-hand again and eased the muzzle into the wall. An intense vibration coursed up his arm, raising the hairs on his forearm and startling him. He withdrew quickly; the tingling sensation faded after a few seconds with no pain.

Jack didn't know what to think of it. The wall was unlike anything he'd ever laid his eyes on. If there was anything inside, the barrier blocked all light and sound from escaping it. *Was* there anything in here? Was it all just vast, empty space?

The thought of stepping into it occurred. He shook it from his mind—after all, he had no idea what could be in there, or if he would survive stepping into it. What if he couldn't breathe? What if the wall—or void, whatever it was—had no floor?

He went down on one knee and placed his palm on soft soil at the edge of the wall. Then, slowly, he slid his left hand toward it. His fingers tingled when they entered the wall, as did his hand when he slid the rest of it in. Hairs stood up again from the electric current that sizzled painlessly through his nerves and tendons. He slid further until the wall had consumed his elbow. His shoulder tickled. The sensation in his arm felt like he'd slept on it all night.

There was a floor.

He couldn't stand it any longer. He didn't want to step into the void; didn't want to chance it just yet. It should be fine, so long as he kept himself anchored in the plains, right? He would only peek through the wall for a moment. He had to know.

266

He had to *see*. He had to know if he *could* see; if it was all dense blackness.

Positioning himself on his knees directly in front of the wall, Jack bent forward. He held his breath, closed his eyes, and dipped his head into the void. He was immediately assaulted with deafening static. A television set left at full volume without a signal. Jack panicked and lurched back out of it, staring at the wall in wide-eyed terror. His nerves were shot. His body trembled furiously.

He sat there for a while, catching his breath, trying to sum up the courage to move. He felt as though the wall would suddenly fall forward and consume him, but it didn't move.

Jack breathed deeply, reassuring himself in his head that he was being irrational. There was nothing here but static. It helped calm his nerves.

His eyes had never opened on the other side. Now that he'd recovered from his initial blind experience with the inside of the void, he cursed himself for his lack of commitment in learning more about this new discovery. He promised himself he would keep his eyes open this time as he reassumed his position in front of the wall. He counted.

One... two... three!

He hesitated. Psyched himself out. "Fuck!" he snarled. He sucked in air, blew it out. "Okay."

One... two...

He thrust his head forward. The static roar filled his ears and his head again; his skull pulsed under his scalp. Jack opened his eyes and saw a narrow underground tunnel that stretched without end to a vanishing point. Its walls were painted scarlet. The floor and ceiling were polished glass that reflected each other in dizzying, kaleidoscopic infinity. At first, Jack thought he was looking into a canyon with red walls and thousands of floors until he looked down and saw himself reflected a thousand times. He couldn't see any special light sources to explain the red hue of the tunnel. There were no spaces for anything to hide in here, which was relieving. But it didn't need anything to occupy it. The space itself struck him with a deep, unshakeable fear. He didn't want to know what was on the other side. Something tried to draw him in further, but

268

he found himself paralyzed with fear. The static was overwhelming. His head ached, his optic nerves throbbing.

It drew him in; the white noise shouted distorted messages in his ears, ensnaring him against his better judgment, against his will. He wasn't in control of his body. He could only move his eyes, which he shifted frantically as he watched himself step into the corridor and walk onto the glass floor. He didn't dare look down. He felt paralyzed, but his legs continued to put one foot in front of the other. His neck was stiff and rigid, his head stuck in a fixed, forward position. His heart pounded in his ears. His eyes watered. The walls seemed to close in the further he walked. His footsteps echoed with surprising intensity, thundering through multiple illusory floors stretching above and below him. His gun-hand liquefied; the revolver slipped through fluid fingers and slammed onto the floor with a shattering report, as if it'd fired a shot. It was a clean break through the static for only a moment.

He left the gun behind. The white noise returned with a vengeance. Cicadas in his head overlapping the deep, rumbling ambience that resonated through the tunnel. The reflections above and below him transformed into abstract things he couldn't describe. He heard things he couldn't place; familiar-sounding old tunes and voices and muffled conversations he remembered having, remembered living through, but he couldn't place them in his mind. They were haunting, gnawing at him. *Where did I hear these things before?*

The tunnel dragged on. Its crimson walls shimmered wetly, as if the paint had only been applied a few hours ago. There was no new paint smell or even an odour of any kind as far as he could tell. Time slowed down with every step, each footfall a deafening echo, a break in the constant static that assaulted him. The tunnel ahead rotated, twisting into a vortex, skewing future reflections of Jack into elongated figures curving around in humanoid, semicircular forms converging on an invisible central point. They all twisted their heads around and glared at their past self, at current Jack. *Keep up, old man. You're too slow.*

Jack still had no control over his own body. It continued to move against him,

270

shuffling forward stiffly, slowly, oh, so painfully slowly.

An intersection soon revealed itself to him. The narrow, one-way corridor was an illusion shattered by this junction. He heard alien sirens and high-pitched distortions in the depths of these other corridors on either side of him, but he still couldn't move his head, and couldn't see where they led. If they led anywhere. His reflection in the floor diverted course, turning left, while his reflection in the ceiling turned right. Their footsteps overlapped, not quite in sync with his own anymore as he left them behind. He continued straight. One of his reflections let out a horrified scream that was abruptly cut off.

Jack gnashed his teeth. He couldn't speak. His lips quivered as they peeled over his teeth. Tears rolled down his face.

Another junction. His reflections split and went their separate ways while he remained on the forward path. He braced himself; his watering eyes squinting, every muscle tensing up as he anticipated a scream.

Something *screeched* like a power

drill scraping down a blackboard. It had that mechanical whine to it. Jack winced from the pain it inflicted on his ears. It only lasted a few seconds, reverberating through the polished glass floor after it'd gone, but it endured in his mind, replaying on a loop in his memory.

Another intersection slinked into his view. Again, he saw his reflection turn into reflections and disappear out of his peripherals while his legs took him forward.

He reached it. Somehow he'd reached the vanishing point, which was not a vanishing point, but a blown-up, wall-to-ceiling photograph of the corridor, a simulation of endlessness. Jack realized he could move his body at will again. He wiped his eyes and his nose on his sleeves and spun around to look back from where he came from. He saw himself, a doppelganger, walking back from where he came from. The doppelganger's backside receded as he calmly retraced his steps toward the only exit he knew.

Jack turned his attention to the paper wall and poked a hole into it with his forefinger. He realized he hadn't heard a scream this time. He tore the paper away,

272

expecting the presence of some unspeakable horror, but instead he found a black emptiness with no floor, no light. More like the wall in the tall grass, but the white noise was deafening now, shrill, resounding endlessly from the depths of the abyss.

He felt like he could reach out and touch it, so he did. His hand vanished. He gasped, pulled back. His hand returned to his wrist. It was just like the first wall.

He bent forward and submerged his face into the mire. He opened his eyes and peered into the void.

When the void in all its shapeless, colourless, sentient enormity looked back at him, he screamed.

Saturday, December 16th, 2000 - Part II

Dan Snr didn't go downstairs. Instead, he turned out of the doorway with his back against the wall. "Cassandra!" She raised her head and peeked at him through the front seat windows. "Go find the keys and get those kids out of here."

"Have you seen Jack?"

Dan Snr shook his head. "Where did you see him last?"

"In the living room."

Dan Snr's heart sank with dread. He took a deep breath and shoved another round into his shotgun. "He can take care of himself. Go find the keys. They're in the foyer somewhere. I'll watch the kids."

"But—"

"*GO*! There isn't time!"

Cassandra knelt down, left the package in Hannah's hands. "Keep that safe." She touched each child's face, cherished it, in case it was the last time she'd ever see them again. "Listen. I'll be right back. Okay? I'm just getting the keys. We're gonna get out of here, okay?"

"Mom, I'm scared," Alistair sobbed.

"Please don't go," Hannah said.

"I will be *right* back," she said.

"Mommy." Snot was dripping from Harry's nose, his little face distended in anguish. "Please, Mommy."

"Hey, hey, now," Cassandra said as soothingly as her trembling voice could manage. She wiped her youngest son's nose on a napkin wad she had pocketed earlier. "I won't be long. Grandpa will take good care of you."

Dan Snr risked a glance into the basement. "What're you doing, Cass? Get going before they storm the house!"

Cassandra ran for it, clearing the steps in a single leap, stumbling into the foyer. She checked the wall hooks. The keys weren't there. She fell to her knees and searched the floor, swiping boots and shoes aside, her anxiety rising with every passing second she couldn't see them. She lifted the rug but the keys weren't under it. She shoved things out of the closet; checked coat pockets, then suddenly thought to check her own pockets. Her fingers touched cold, jagged metal. Her heart flared. "Oh God, I had them... Marcy... I had them this whole time... I forgot... oh, God, I forgot..."

She looked toward the kitchen door. Snow was drifting in through the windows, crystal flakes riding along with the swirling draft through the devastated kitchen and beyond. She could see abstract shadows dancing on the walls and floors, cast by the flickering glow of the television. "Jack...?" She heard wet crunching sounds, slopping noises; things that she'd never heard before. Like mud sucking a boot into its depths, snapping twigs hidden beneath the surface.

She saw a face hanging upside down. Marcy's eyes were vacant; her head past her hairline was missing; her neck was reduced to a few fleshy strands swinging it back and forth from a half-eaten torso suspended above the floor by two pairs of rotted hands.

The revenants' fingers were abnormally long, curled around Marcy's remains like the upended legs of dead spiders. The TV's harsh glow created black, sinewy veins in the grooves of the rotting, distorted meat that stretched over their inhuman bone structures. The things that engorged themselves on Marcy's

276

organs hadn't noticed her sister-in-law watching them.

It took everything in her not to scream at the sight of them. She staggered away, gripping the keys in a shaking fist, not daring to turn around, instead backing toward the garage. Her eyes were wide as saucers. Tears dripped from her chin. Her lips quivered as they peeled back, showing her teeth gritted in terrified revulsion. Her breath caught in her throat. Her chest shuddered convulsively as she struggled to breathe.

Dan Snr shouted from the garage. "Cassandra!"

The revenants heard him. Warped heads with glowing white eyes swung up and around on long necks to gaze at Cassandra, as deer startled from their grazing would. Marcy's face slipped from the jaws of John's revenant and slapped the floor. John, a thing, not the in-law she once knew, but a horrible adaptation of his likeness if it had been carelessly molded by a child. Those same eyes from the window held her in a penetrating gaze that seemed to mock her, while something else hissed at her from within the jagged pit in the center of his face. Something that *squirmed* in the black, exposed recesses of his skull, scraping around in his head with burrowing claws and a slug-like body.

No. Not a slug—a *centipede* with a toothy, human grin. It crawled out of John's face, its hundred-thousand tiny little legs shimmering in the glow of the TV as it snaked down and around John's torso and his left leg to the floor.

Cassandra heard its legs pitter-patter on the floor and disturb the debris there. "No." She threw the foyer door shut, shaking glass shards out of their panes, and scrambled back into the garage. She yelled at the children, "Get in the car!" as she unlocked the doors with the key fob. She slammed the foyer door behind her, its vertical window still intact. She risked breaking a leg or an ankle by leaping off the stairs, landed rightly, bounded round the front of the car to scoop up Harry. "Come on, baby." She opened the driver side door and deposited Harry on Martin's lap in the passenger seat as Hannah, Brian, and Alistair climbed into the back seats. "Strap yourselves in. Now." The children started to protest, asking questions, frightened and

278

confused. "Not now!" She raised her head above the roof and said to Dan Snr, who was still standing by the basement door, "I couldn't find Jack. Those same things are in the living room! I-I don't know what they are; they were... they were eating—"

"Don't worry about it, just go!" Dan Snr saw the fear and pain on her face and softened his tone slightly. "We'll be fine, Cass. Get them outta here."

Cassandra hesitated. She wanted to go back in. She wanted to find Jack, drag him out away from those things if they hadn't already...

"Cassandra, *GO!*"

She banged the roof of the car with her fist and then fell in behind the wheel. She started it up, engine grumbling to life, and then she raised the garage rollers with a button-push on the key fob—

Hannah started screaming at the top of her lungs between the seats.

Marcus, without legs, his skin charred and bubbled and cratered from the blazing crash, fully illuminated in the car's headlights, hung by his neck in a Christmas light noose. His mouth hung open in a silent scream. His eyes were reduced to black pits dribbling white puss down the spiraling grooves in his misshapen face. His arms were extended toward them in a manner befitting someone who feared death.

Blinding light filled the garage, turning Marcus into an abstract shape. A low-frequency sound hummed seemingly from everywhere, its nauseating drone disorienting Cassandra, the children, and Dan Snr.

Six cultists materialized from the light in two-by-two formation, black shapes assuming humanoid forms as they flanked Marcus's revenant and the car with their faces behind gas masks, their heads encased in televisions and headsets. Their shadows danced all over the garage, further confusing Dan Snr, who fell to his knees, overtaken by the cicadas buzzing around in his skull. He could feel them tickling his optic nerves.

The cultists attacked.

Shadows danced ritualistically all over the garage interior. Metallic hooting and screeching and giggling was amplified by the garage's small space. The crashing sound of shattering glass was louder.

The cultists smashed the side windows of the car, spraying the passengers' faces with glass. One of them drove a pole through Cassandra's window and shattered her cheekbone, snapping her head toward the passenger seat. Another one thrust his spade into the back seat, sheering skin off the tip of Brian's nose. The children shrieked and tried to flatten themselves against the seats.

Dan Snr gritted his teeth; their screams forced him to try to get a grip. He aimed at a flickering shadow from his perspective. His shotgun roared from behind the car, peppering fragments of the left side of the cultist's masked head onto his companions, his spade slackening across the back seat. The spade impeded the efforts of a cultist with a hatchet trying to pull Alistair out of the opposite window.

Another cultist between the blinding light and the hatchet-man dragged Harry off Martin's lap through the passenger window and flung the screaming child over the stairs. He hit the wall by the fridge and stopped screaming. He bounced against the freezer box and tumbled onto the floor like a ragdoll.

Dan Snr staggered against the wall, jacking another round into his shotgun and squinting against the dizziness caused by the frequency. He heard Alistair crying and fired at the hatchet-man, ripped his torso into a gaping mouth from which his steaming organs spilled. The round blew through the hatchet-man and the passenger seat.

Cassandra's ears were filled with a high-pitched squeal. She was blinded by white light and white-hot agony. She tried to scream but choked on blood and teeth instead. Instinctively she floored the gas. The car lurched forward. Marcus slapped against the windshield and disappeared over the car, leaving only the light. The car jolted. Someone was flung across the hood. She hit something, she knew. A cultist fell under the car and curled up in the wheel well. The tire shredded his electrical tape outfit and the feeble flesh beneath. The television set he wore interrupted the cycle. The TV helmet crumpled around the loosely connected head. The tire jammed. The car fishtailed across the gravel lot, spraying the cultist's organs out of the wheel well in an arc, forming a bright red crescent of gore in the snow.

The car broadsided Officer Jameson's cruiser, hurling the children across the back seat, and kept going. Cassandra's head fell against the seat pad. Her eyes rolled back, bleeding profusely from the shattered left side of her face.

The car rammed into a tree. Cassandra vaulted forward, blasting through the windshield across the hood, arms outstretched. Snow plopped down from shaken branches, covering her and the hissing engine block that was now wrapped around the tree's trunk.

The cultists guffawed mockingly at the wreck until a high-pitched wail echoed from the basement. Synchronized, they all turned and looked straight at Dan Snr.

Dan Snr huddled in the corner with the shotgun in his left hand, his right arm raised to shield his eyes from the light until it was inexplicably turned off in the next moment. He rubbed his eyes quickly, eager to keep them in his sights, and looked back at them. Three were left standing in the garage. Twenty more emerged from the woods to join them. Television sets, gas masks, night vision goggles, and improvised helmets coiled thickly in loose microchips, computer mice, even keyboards all threaded together with spools of computer cords. They all carried weapons; knives, hatchets, baseball bats, lead pipes, bars, chains, flamethrowers, and chainsaws.

Donna Anderson stepped out of the basement, now walking on long, lithe legs to face them. Bare feet slapped wetly on the concrete floor. Dan Snr noticed they were leaving red footprints. Her naked body was spattered with Officer Jameson's blood. Her stomach was swollen, giving her the appearance of a pregnant woman. She didn't shiver in the cold. In fact, she seemed to enjoy it. She exhaled like a habitual smoker, her breath pluming in the stiff, chill air.

The frequency's broadcast ended as suddenly as it began. Dan Snr was left panting as he recovered from waves of nausea and dizziness. He lay against the wall, still struggling to get his bearings. Sweaty fists gripped the shotgun.

The smoke detectors blared from within the house. Smoke rolled in from the foyer, filling the garage with a thin, grey haze.

284

The cult members advanced with their weapons pointed toward Donna Anderson. Calmly, she swept her right arm in a wide arc; an invisible force lifted one of them off the floor, slammed him into the wall next to the basement door. The crack of his spine shattering with the force was almost as loud as Dan Snr's shotgun.

Another cultist swung his pickaxe at her head, but inexplicably froze in mid-swing. He gasped in horror, trying to finish the killing blow, but his limbs didn't respond to his mental commands. Donna Anderson snapped her fingers. The cultist turned the pickaxe on himself, then pitched himself onto it, landing flat on the floor. The point burst through his back. He gurgled, legs kicking uselessly as a pool of blood spread from under him.

A chainsaw howled as a third cultist charged her. He made it two feet, then twirled with balletic graze and leaped weightlessly back toward the others. The chainsaw whined as its teeth ripped its way through the torso of his nearest companion, splattering the screaming cultist's insides all over their surrounding comrades.

The others didn't get a chance to

react. They were no longer in control. The cultists slaughtered each other, helpless against Donna Anderson's psychokinetic commands. They hacked each other with hatchets, slashed limbs with knives; organs gushed out, arteries sprayed, heads made sucking noises as axe-wielders struggled to pull their weapons out of them.

Dan Snr watched in horror as the maelstrom of violence continued to unfold before him. The deafening melee filled the garage with a hellish orchestra of crashing and screaming. Arterial spray streaked the walls and rafters. Blood and gore splashed across concrete. Heads and limbs bounced and rolled. Flex ductwork tore. TVs smashed. Electrical tape ripped. Computer parts shattered. Bones splintered under penetrated flesh. Their numbers shrank from double digits to single digits in a matter of seconds. The last of them grappled with each other, weapons abandoned in favour of their own fists and hands, slipping and sliding on a steaming lake of mutilated corpses. They tripped over their fallen dead and collapsed, entangled in their desperate struggle to survive, to beat their fellow man.

To be free of their restrictive flesh.

Donna Anderson applauded their performance, cheering them on like a mother would support their child at an extracurricular sports event. Four remained. One of them was shoved between two bodies. He snatched a knife from a dead man's hand and stuck its blade through his attacker's jugular. Blood sprayed his goggles as his attacker, a heavyset man, sagged on top of him. The knife-wielder wriggled under the corpse as another cultist ripped the cord on his chainsaw. The tool roared to life. The pinned-down man screamed at the top of his lungs, begging his friend to stop. His friend screamed endless apologies, his eyes wet with tears as he plunged the chainsaw through the heavyset man's back, eventually reaching the man under it. Crimson geysers erupted, splattering the rafters, the single window along the side, the tools hung up on the wall, the jerry cans by the work bench, and Donna Anderson.

The man with the chainsaw couldn't see through the wild blood spray that drenched him. He couldn't see the second-last cultist behind him either, and never did,

287

as the semi-final man crept up behind him and plunged a screwdriver into his ear before they were both engulfed in flaming napalm from the flamethrower man who killed John's revenant. Standing in the garage entrance, he torched everything within ten feet of him—the bodies of his companions, Marcus's revenant dangling from the eavestrough, the stairs leading up to the foyer, and little Harry's body.

The roller doors dropped down on him suddenly, pinning him to the ground. Liquid fire spewed from his flamethrower, scorched the rafters, dropped back down on him. He flailed and howled as he drowned in his own flames.

Dan Snr stared at Donna's backside as the scene inexplicably changed; the garage narrowed, triggering claustrophobic terror that Dan Snr hadn't realized he had. His vision was saturated with red light. The floor and ceiling became clear surfaces that reflected each other hundreds of times. Donna Anderson's lithe figure multiplied above and below, upside down and right side up, stuttering before his eyes like a film reel. He blinked several times until he was back in the garage.

288

Donna turned to face Dan Snr, her expression bright with twisted amusement, as the cultists melted in the raging inferno. Intense heat burst the ceiling lights.

"Why?" he asked her.

"They were idiots," she replied coldly. "The world is full of them. Gullible... impressionable... susceptible to a beautiful woman's shallow charms and empty promises. Like you," she added, striding toward him. "There's no shortage of them. More will come. There will *always* be more."

He didn't hesitate. Dan Snr raised his shotgun and blasted a hole through her stomach. Portions of Officer Jameson slid out of her and hit the ground in wet, gnarly clumps. Her stomach shrank down again, gnarly portions of stretched skin curling into frilly edges around the hole.

She looked down with annoyance. "That wasn't very gentlemanly of y—"

Dan Snr jacked another round in and aimed higher, pulled the trigger. The shotgun bucked in his hands. He watched her head snap around, chunks of her jaw spinning into the inferno behind her. Her tongue flapped against her throat like a necktie. Blood gushed down her front from her pitted flesh below her upper teeth, some of which had been knocked out of place.

The tank of the flamethrower ruptured, launching the roller door into the driveway and hurling a pillar of liquid fire into the rafters where it pooled and spread above Donna Anderson's imposing figure. Her eyes flared with white-hot rage. Her chest heaved as she inhaled deeply with a grated, bubbling noise. Blood seeped out of pitted clumps of hanging meat where her jaw used to be with every ragged breath she took, cascading between her breasts and down her stomach. Her new glistening, crimson corset left nothing to the imagination.

Dan Snr pumped his shotgun once more, knowing what was coming. She was impervious, but he was defiant. He aimed.

She clenched her left fist.

His head imploded.

290

Saturday, December 16th, 2000 - Part III

It was a little square portal like the one before; a window into his parents' house. The smoke was too thick; the heat surging from it blew across his face, stinging his eyes. The walls and mirrored floor and ceiling had fluttered away like plumes of confetti, revealing the grass field around him as if he'd never left.

He couldn't remember how he got here. A gap in his memory erased his return to the plains.

Jack retreated helplessly away from the portal, a flickering orange square hovering above the grass, belching black plumes into the air.

Jack heard laughter drifting with the breeze from somewhere else. He whirled, trying to locate its source. The plains and the shoreline were still devoid of all life. Cameron Morgan's revenant hadn't moved from where it'd collapsed; dark wisps of smoke continued to drift from its charred corpse. The swirling clouds were alive with dancing shadows flailing their abnormally

291

long limbs, and a hideous laughter peeled across the plains.

Jack could still hear the buzzing white noise in his skull, only now it was faintly comforting in comparison to his first encounter with it. He turned and looked back at the vast, black wall, but it wasn't there. Nothing was there, but he could hear it. He could hear the Noise. He could feel it. He felt as though he had become a part of it.

He studied his hands in silent awe. They were perfectly intact; his right hand was free of the gun and the wounds that occurred when it was fused to his bones.

He returned his attention to the portal. The heat of the inferno on the other side intensified. Smoke obscured everything the fire hadn't already devoured. He stood directly in front of the portal, breathing in the choking fumes that filtered into the crisp, summer air.

Jack crossed the plain, headed away from the shore, the portal, and the space where the vast wall once occupied. He could hear shouts coming from behind a grassy hill, so he ascended the hill, and as he descended the other side, the tall grass shriveled and died around him, clearing a path that revealed another portal. It was a window to a tranquil scene of undisturbed snow and trees.

Jack approached it cautiously. He glanced with furtive alertness toward every direction he could see through the opening, studying every dark shadow, every shape in the dark forest.

Then he jumped through and suddenly found himself surrounded by cultists with nets and a variety of weapons. The spider-cultist loomed over him, its hissing breath pluming from both sides of its mask. They appeared out of nowhere!

Jack sprang up like a rabbit and took off through the trees past the other cultists before they could strike him down. Gouts of liquid fire chased him, its stream broken by the trees he passed. He reached the trail between the shed and the house. He gasped in horror at the sight of the pillar of fire billowing up from the collapsing hips and valleys of the house's roof. The brick walls were blackening. The inferno reached thirty feet into the early morning sky, turning night into flickering day, washing the entire surrounding property in an apocalyptic red haze. Jack could feel the heat sixty feet up the trail.

The scene of carnage in the driveway—all those bodies and black-red Rorschach patterns of gore that stained the snow—caught his attention next.

And then Donna Anderson, still naked and standing silhouetted in the flames billowing angrily out of the garage, struck him with paralyzing fear. She was holding Dan Snr's shotgun against her thigh.

It was all the cultists needed to catch him by surprise. They threw a bag over his head, latched a catchpole around his neck, and slammed him to the ground. They'd choked a scream out of him before he could make one. He wriggled in protest, in desperate terror, gurgling as more of them rushed him, shocking him with a stun baton and binding his hands together while the other end of the catchpole was attached to the spider-cultist's belt. They towed Jack down the trail away from the house as he kicked up snow and gravel.

Donna Anderson's unblinking eyes watched them recede into the dark forest. The cultists had abandoned their mission.

294

She was free to eat the children now.

She gagged on her own blood, spurting it out of her throat where her lower jaw used to be, as she started limping toward the crashed car. When she reached it, she bent forward, peered into the back seat. The door on the driver's side was open. The back seat was empty. No package. No children. She released a guttural snarl and checked the front seats. There was a hole in the front passenger seat from a shotgun blast; little Martin's head mostly painted the dash, now. Cassandra was slumped over the wheel, her arms and head outstretched under a pile of snow on the hood. Donna saw that she was twitching. She stepped forward, raised the shotgun with her left arm and blasted Cassandra's head off of the hood. An explosion of snow, windshield fragments, and Jack's wife filled the air momentarily. The shot echoed through the forest. Donna staggered beyond the tree the car was wrapped around and found three sets of little footprints in the snow leading to the road.

She pumped the shotgun, coughed another spurt from her mangled throat, and trudged up the driveway.

*

Hannah had woken up first. She was hugging the package her aunt had given her. She tucked the package under her coat, making sure it was secured in the waistband of her snow pants.

The driveway was alive with a brutal melee and the house was burning. She snapped back into reality and shook Alistair and Brian awake. "Wake up! Wake up!" She moved up to the front seat. "Martin—"

Martin's body lay inert in the passenger seat. The dashboard glistened grotesquely in the fire's light. Hannah burst into tears and retched, turning away. Cassandra's body split her heart in half. An agonizing whine droned out of her, escalating to a scream. *"AUNTIE!"*

By now, Alistair had come to. "Mom?" he groaned, rubbing a fresh welt on his head and grimacing at its tenderness. "Mom? Where's Mom?"

"No!" Hannah shrieked, trying to block Alistair's view of the front seat. "Don't look!"

"Why?" More alert now, Alistair tried to shove her out of his way. "Where's

296

Mom? Martin?" He checked Brian, who was still coming out of a pained daze. "Where're my brothers? Martin? Harry? *Mom*?"

"No, Al, trust me, please—"

A cultist's body smashed through the rear window. All three children screamed and shielded themselves from falling glass. Somehow the chaos outside was much louder now. Brian whimpered and was the first to crawl out of the car, falling into snow that reached his elbows.

Hannah tumbled backwards against the radio, her feet kicking between the seats, hitting Alistair's shoulder as he clambered out after Brian. Hannah was the last one out, running past Alistair, who'd stopped to try and shake his mother awake.

"Mom? You okay? Mom?"

Hannah came back and grabbed his shoulders. "Al, please—we have to go."

"Fuck off!" Alistair swiped her arms away. He continued to shake Cassandra's arm. "Mom!" he blubbered, as it truly sank in. He caught a glimpse of Martin's headless body in the passenger seat, with no sign of Harry, and opened his mouth to scream. Hannah slapped her hand over his mouth and tackled him to the ground.

"Be quiet! Please, Al!" she begged through her own tears. "You have to stay strong."

Alistair struggled and screamed into her hand, his cursing muffled. He bit her but she held on. He flailed violently, hitting his cousin, the car, the ground, and even himself as he tried to wriggle free of her grasp, but Hannah persisted.

Brian had already reached the road and started off toward town without looking back.

Snow flew around Hannah and Alistair as she struggled to contain his raging sorrow. Their noises were drowned out by the din on the other side, but the chaos was beginning to subside as Donna Anderson systematically wiped them out.

"We have to go." Hannah was trying to get through to him. "We have to go, Al. Come on. We can't stay here. She'll kill us!"

"I don't care! Get off me!" He wriggled under her. She held on. He was slowing down, exhausting himself with the exertion. He sagged into the snow and sobbed, trembling.

298

"I know it hurts, Al. Trust me, I know. But we can't stay here. we have to go, Al. We have to go while she's distracted. Or we'll wind up like everybody else. Do you want that? Do you? Al?"

"No," Alistair said. He'd stopped struggling, but the trembling continued. Hannah realized he wasn't the only one.

"Then get up." She forced herself to sound angry, to sound stronger than she really was, like all those cool heroines on TV, the ones who could karate-kick a man twice their size out of a high-rise window from across the room. The ones who showed no fear in the face of death. The ones who ran back into the Alien Queen's lair if it meant saving a child before the countdown to oblivion reached zero.

"Get up *right now*," she growled in his ear. "If we die here, I'll never forgive you. Wipe your face, Al."

He wiped his face on his coat sleeve. Snot stuck to his arm. Suddenly self-conscious, he rubbed snow on it. Still sniffling, he took her hand and let her tow him through the front yard, leaving the sounds of death and destruction behind

299

them.

The road was unlit, barren, stretching several kilometres in either direction. Brian's winter coat was a bobbing red apple in the distance. The house continued to burn, casting long, animated shadows across the road. Hannah and Alistair chased Brian, their gloved hands stuck together. As they left the property behind, the firelight faded, as did the screams.

The moon peeked over the trees, mostly hidden from sight. Darker shades of blue spilled across the sky in its absence. The snow reflected what little moonlight remained, providing the children with a clear enough sense of direction. Their boots clomped loudly on sludge-smothered concrete. Their snow pants scraped together as they ran. Brian had had a good head start, but he was slowing down, allowing them to catch up, and when they did Hannah released Alistair's hand and used it to swat her brother across the head. His orange snowcap flew into the ditch.

"Ow!" Brian whined as he turned and glared at her. He rubbed the back of his head. "What the hell!"

Hannah was fuming. "Some brother

you are! We almost died back there! What the hell is wrong with you?"

"Screw you! You guys got out just fine without me babysitting you."

Hannah shoved him off the road and watched him tumble to the bottom of the ditch. He splashed through a thin layer of ice and set himself upright in a shallow pool of murky water. Brian started to cry. "Serves you right, you big loser!"

Alistair glanced back down the road. He could still see the house's orange glow in the distance.

Brian retrieved his hat, growling in his throat. He clawed his way back up to the road and punched his sister in the arm.

"Ow!" She tried to counter. He shoved her onto the road for her troubles.

"Bitch! I hope they kill you, too! When I get older I'm gonna come back here for revenge, but I'll only avenge Mom and Dad, not *you*, because you suck!" Brian turned and continued on his way along the road, stomping his feet. "See ya, losers!"

Alistair stared at his cousin as she sat upright, fighting tears. He extended his hand. "You okay?"

She wiped her eyes and sniffed. She

took his hand and let him help her to her feet. "Yeah, I'm okay."

"Somebody else's gotta live on this street, too, right?" Alistair said. "Maybe they can help us."

"Stranger danger, Al. We don't know what they could do to us in their houses."

"Can't be worse than..."

She fixed him with a sad look and stuck her hands in her coat pockets. "Come on. Let's go."

They caught up to Brian as soon as the next house came into view. It was a bungalow set behind intricate Christmas decorations—a life-size recreation of the birth of Jesus haloed with green and red blinking lights. No lights were on in the house.

Hannah smacked Brian's arm, still feeling angry about earlier. "Wait."

"No, *you* wait. Wait to get eaten or whatever."

"Stop, you idiot." She pointed at the house. "They might have a phone."

Brian scanned the property. "If they're even home. I don't wanna go into some stranger's house, anyway. What if whoever lives there is weird?"

302

"Then we'll run away before they can get us," Alistair said.

Brian scoffed. "Sure, doofus. You'll be the first one they get."

"Knock it off," Hannah snapped. "Why do you have to be such a dick?"

Brian's eyes flared. "Feel free to go back there and ask! I didn't invite you to come with me, anyway."

Hannah clicked her tongue, hesitating. She shivered in the cold. "I'm gonna go knock on the door."

Alistair asked, "I thought you didn't wanna do that?"

"I'm cold."

"What if there's a rapist in there?" Brian asked, mockingly.

"I'll tell him where you sleep so that you get raped first," she hissed.

"No, *you're* getting raped first! In the butt!"

Alistair stood there, listening to the siblings bicker with increasing ferocity. There wasn't an end to it in sight, and it was beginning to irritate him. Alistair felt like his dad must have felt—he always seemed to be annoyed with the children in his presence. Alistair understood, at least to

303

some degree, as his cousins continued to argue. He heaved a deep sigh and started down the driveway toward the bungalow. "Screw this."

The siblings stopped bickering.

"Al!"

"Where're you going?"

"I'm gonna see if anyone's home and ask to use their phone."

"Don't do it," Brian yelled.

"Who would we even call?" Hannah asked.

"The cops, maybe?"

"I mean, maybe," Hannah said.

"But what if you get raped?" Brian asked.

"Boys don't get raped," Alistair said. "That's why Hannah should stay outside."

"That's not true! Al!" Hannah ran down the driveway after him.

Brian looked down both ends of the road. Suddenly he felt very exposed and vulnerable out here. "Wait for me." He followed them, making sure he was at least three steps away from them in case there was a serial killer in the house.

"I watched a documentary about how boys in the Vatican were being used by

304

priests and stuff," Hannah said. "Plus, statistically speaking, most boys don't report that stuff because they wanna look strong or whatever."

Brian snickered.

"What's so funny?"

"Real men don't get raped. But girls are super weak and helpless, so it happens to them all the time."

They reached the attached garage at the end of the driveway and started up the path to the doorstep. Icicles lined the eavestrough like a row of jagged teeth.

"*Wow*, jerk-face. Is that why you're hiding behind me, a *weak, helpless* little girl? Sure says something about you. Alistair's more of a man than you'll ever be. I wish he was my brother instead."

"Shh!" Alistair hissed at them. Before his cousins could respond, light appeared in the window above them. They froze, fearful, as a screen door squeaked open. An old man leaned out, his slender frame wrapped in a dark housecoat. He had a nightcap on. His face was shriveled and gentle. When he saw the children, he squinted in disbelief, stepped out in his slippers and shivered in the morning chill,

305

leaning on a cane.

"What the hell're you kids doin' out here this early in the morning? Why're you on my property? Who *are* you? You Delia's kids? Speak up!"

Alistair was petrified. He couldn't bring himself to speak. Brian remained hidden behind his sister, hoping he hadn't already been seen.

Hannah answered the old man from behind Alistair. "Sorry, sir. We're not from here. We were... w-we were vising our grandma when someone attacked the house and—" she burst into tears without warning. Not even she could have stopped them. "We didn't know what else to do!"

The old man stared at them with utter confusion on his face. He turned with great effort as a woman's voice called out from inside, "Harold, what is it?"

"It's kids," he answered. "Three of 'em."

There was a pause. "It's three in the morning."

"Yeah, tell *them* that."

Hannah said, "We just need a phone to call somebody."

"Where are their parents?" the

306

woman's voice asked.

"Beats me." The old man called Harold asked the kids directly, "Where are your parents?"

"They're dead!" Alistair blurted, and then he started crying, too.

Brian wiped his eyes on his sleeve, not wanting anyone to see that he was doing the same thing.

The woman must have heard their moaning, because she hurried out in her boots and pink nightie to see what all the commotion was about. "Oh, my God! Harold!" She turned to her husband. "Harold, why didn't you let them in? What's wrong with you?"

Harold shrugged, lifting his cane as he did so. He was at a loss for words.

"Come inside, dears. It's too cold out. Come inside, now."

The kids hesitated.

"We won't hurt you." The woman's voice was soft and consoling. "If Harold tries to give you beer, just kick his cane out from under him. That always works for me!"

"You never did that, Sarah, don't give 'em ideas," Harold grumbled. "Kids these days're bad enough. I ain't sharing my goddamn beer with any kids."

The elderly couple watched the kids cry on their front step for only a few seconds more. It was longer than either of them could bear.

"Come in, now," Sarah said, approaching them slowly. "I'll make you some hot chocolate, if you like. Warm yourselves by our fireplace. It's not a real fireplace, mind you; one of those electric ones, but it does the trick." She reached them and touched Hannah's shoulder, bending forward so that her face was level with hers. "You're safe, now. Children your age shouldn't be out this late, especially when it's this cold."

Hannah let Sarah lead her inside. The boys quickly followed, not willing to let her go alone with these people. Harold was the last one inside. He scanned the road for any signs of life, and when he saw none, he shut the screen door and locked it. He peered through the screen once again, as a precaution, and then closed the main door.

The house was kept at a comfortable temperature. The children could feel themselves thawing in its warm embrace. It

308

smelled a little like Wilma and Dan Snr's house. That strange elderly smell. Doilies seemed to be everywhere, along with framed pictures of friends, relatives, children, and grandchildren on the walls. A few paintings and old medals from accomplishments met in another life. The kids left their boots on a mostly empty rack and then crossed the kitchen's white linoleum floor to the living room carpet. Once there, Harold tinkered with the electric fireplace, cursing it under his breath until it turned on. The children sat down in front of it.

Sarah came in with a pile of quilted blankets folded in her arms. She asked Harold, "Are all the doors locked?"

Harold nodded.

"You're sure?"

Harold thought for a moment. "I'll check."

As he set out to check the back door in the next room, Sarah distributed the blankets among the children.

"Where's your phone?" Hannah asked.

Sarah led her to a small table next to the couch where a red landline rested.

Hannah picked up the receiver and started dialing for the police before she realized there was no dial tone. Complete silence.

"The line's dead," she stated.

Sarah furrowed her eyebrows. She put the receiver to her ear. Perplexed, she checked the wires. "That's strange. Harold!"

"The doors are all locked. I'm sure of it." He came out of the back room. "I just checked."

"The phone's not working."

Harold sighed. "Is it plugged in?"

"Yes, it's plugged in. I'm not a fool. The line's dead."

Hannah backed away as Harold lowered himself on one knee with great effort to check the wiring under the little table. "Yep, it's plugged in, alright."

"Yes, I just said that." Sarah's voice sounded firmly annoyed. "Did you pay the bill this month?"

"Of course I paid the bill. I haven't missed a payment in twenty-five goddamn years."

"Language."

"Ahh," he groaned. "They heard worse."

"Not in my house, they won't."

Harold muttered something under his breath as he turned and hobbled into the kitchen.

"What was that?" Sarah asked, setting down the receiver.

"It's automatic."

"What is?"

"The bill payment. It's automatically withdrawn from my account. No way I'm too broke to pay the phone bill. I haven't missed a payment in twenty-five god—in twenty-five years."

"Well, make sure it's stayed that way."

"No way to check till the morning. The bank is closed."

Sarah decided to leave it at that for now. She addressed the children once again and asked, "Would any of you like some hot chocolate?"

Alistair raised his hand. "Me, please."

Hannah asked, "Could I have a tea?"

"Certainly." Sarah leaned toward Brian, who sat the farthest away from her. "What about you?"

"No thanks."

"Harold!"

"What!"

"Don't get snippy with me. Can you get the kettle started?"

"Yeah, I guess so. How much should I fill it?"

"I'd like a tea too, please," Sarah said. Make enough for all of us just in case this one changes his mind."

"Okay."

The children heard water running. Sarah took a seat in a rocking chair on the other side of the room and draped a shawl over her shoulders. Her back faced a picture window overlooking the front yard with a translucent curtain pulled in front of it. "Now," she began, "is anyone able to tell me the circumstances that brought you three here?"

None of them wanted to retell what they went through, so they stared at her with freshly shell-shocked faces. Strangely enough, Sarah seemed to understand. "Harold."

"What?" he yelled over running water.

"Are the windows locked?"

"Goddamn it, there's only one of me.

312

Let me get the kettle goin'."

"Hurry it up."

He appeared to have sensed the new edge in his wife's voice, because he went on with his task without another word. Once he set the kettle down and hit the switch on the stove's gas burner, he disappeared down the hall to the other end of the house. They could hear his cane tapping on the hardwood floor.

Sarah leaned forward on her knees, her expression serious. "Are you in trouble?"

The children exchanged looks that the old woman couldn't comprehend. Eventually, Alistair said, "We don't know."

Hannah added, "We ran away."

"You ran away from home?"

"Well… sort of," Hannah replied. "There were these men in black. Some of them wore TVs and stuff. They played this horrible music a-and there was this man who screamed and destroyed everything in the house, and my mom—"

Sensing another wave of tears, Sarah raised her hand and gently shushed her. "It's alright, child. You're safe now. Where did you three come from?"

"We were visiting our grandma and grandpa," Brian said.

"Who are your grandma and grandpa?"

"Wilma and Dan."

"Oh! You're Jack and Cassandra's kids! Or... are you Marcy and John's kids? Right, I remember seeing a photograph of you. I could have sworn there were more grandkids than just you. Gosh, I can't even remember all of your names."

The children felt a little more at ease after hearing their parents' names. This elderly couple may not have been so strange after all.

She pointed at Alistair. "Is your name Marcus? Are you Marcy and Junior's boy?"

Alistair shook his head. "I'm Jack's oldest. Alistair. Everyone calls me Al."

"Well, Al, it's nice to meet you. And you must be Hannah."

Hannah couldn't stop herself from smiling, at least for a moment. "Yes, ma'am."

"And you must be Brian. Yes, I remember your picture. Wilma was showing me pictures of you all from the last

314

year you visited. You've all grown up so much in so little time. It's nice to finally meet you. But... where are they now? Wilma isn't the type to just let her grandchildren wander around at night. And only a few of you, at that. Did they get separated from you, somehow?"

"They're dead," Alistair said bluntly. "Everyone's dead."

Sarah didn't say anything. She stared at their faces, unsure of how to process what she'd heard. "That's impossible. I just spoke with her over the phone last night. I just... we were discussing cookie recipes..." Her voice trailed off.

They all fell silent, now. The only sounds in the room were the humming of the electric fireplace and the hissing of boiling water on the stove.

Sarah noticed that she couldn't hear Harold's cane tapping on the floor. "Harold?"

No response.

"Harold!"

"What!"

"What are you doing?"

"Fixing the window. The latch wouldn't turn. It's fine, now. I got it."

315

"The kettle's going to boil over."

"Yeah, yeah, I'm listening for it." The cane started tapping toward them. When it touched kitchen linoleum, its sound became blunter. The kettle began to squeal. Harold lifted it off of the stove and turned off the burner. They listened to him place five mugs on the countertop and fill one of them with spoonfuls of hot chocolate powder. He tore the paper wrappers off of two tea bags and dropped them into two mugs. He dropped a spoonful of instant coffee into another mug; the grounds sounded like tiny pebbles cascading through a drainage tunnel. He poured steaming water into each one, stirred them all with the same metal spoon.

"Sarah, bring them over to the table, here."

"Why can't they sit at the fireplace?"

"I don't want 'em spilling anything on our carpet."

"The poor things are exhausted and freezing, Harold."

"Fine." He didn't sound too happy about it.

Sarah went into the kitchen and returned with all their mugs, sans Harold's,

316

on a tray. She asked Hannah if she wanted milk or sugar with her tea.

"No. Thank you." Hannah took her mug graciously.

Alistair lifted his hot chocolate off the tray and thanked Sarah.

Sarah asked Brian, "Are you sure you don't want anything?"

Brian nodded.

"Alright." Sarah returned to her chair and blew steam from the top of her tea. "Be careful. It's very hot."

Harold made his way to the couch. He strained as he bent down, placed his mug on a coaster, and lowered himself onto the seat cushion with a deep exhale.

"Harold," Sarah said.

"I just sat down," he protested.

"I don't need anything," she said. "These are Wilma and Dan's grandkids."

"Ohh," he said, his features lighting up. "How's Dan doing?"

"Not well," Sarah replied, gravely.

"Why? What happened?"

"It's bad. I don't want to get into details with you right now. Not in front of them. But it's bad. And the fact that our phone isn't working has got me feeling a little anxious. It's a little too coincidental, don't you think?"

"It's winter," he said. "It's probably a downed powerline."

"Maybe."

"What's wrong, Sarah?"

"I just think we should drive into town a little earlier than usual today."

"Why?"

"Just a feeling."

"You and your feelings."

"They've never done us wrong before, have they?" When he didn't give her an immediate response, she leaned forward. "*Have* they?"

"No, but…"

"'No, but' what? Harold, I think these children are in danger. And we might be, too, if we don't do something soon."

Harold sipped his instant coffee.

"Harold?"

"I'm thinkin'. Can't a man think?"

"You think too slowly."

They all sat in silence, listening to Harold slurp his coffee.

Something pounded three times against the front door, startling them all.

318

Saturday, December 16th, 2000 - Part IV

A closed fist clubbed the door three more times. The children didn't dare move or make a sound. Sarah and Harold stared at each other. Harold's gaze shifted to the window behind his wife. Sarah's face went pale. She got up out of her chair and hurried toward the kitchen, signalling for the children to follow her. "This way," she whispered. "We'll hide you downstairs until they've gone."

She herded them into the kitchen and then the foyer just as the door shuddered from another assault. "This way. Second door on your right. That's it." A door across from the bathroom revealed a staircase leading down into the basement. The children held the rail as they descended, spilling their drinks on the steps. Sarah closed the door once the last one touched the floor, leaving them in almost pitch darkness. Tiny rectangular windows filtered streams of dim blue light into the fully furnished basement that ran the entire length of the bungalow. It was filled with things from past decades that had no other uses except to collect dust. Two spare guest bedrooms lined the wall behind the stairs. A spare restroom with just a toilet and sink was directly under the staircase. Old marionettes on strings dangling from the ceiling rafters.

The children groped their way through the darkness, tripping over things, spilling their drinks as they caught their ankles around chair and table legs.

The pounding continued—followed by a crack, then something hammering into the floor. Screaming. An earth-shaking boom. Dust showered the children. A thud. Something dragged, and something thumped, then something dragged, then thumped, dragged, thumped...

The children heard Harold's voice distinctly call out, "Sarah?" They heard his cane tapping on the kitchen floor directly above them toward the dragging and the thumping. Another explosion. Hannah thought the ceiling would suddenly drop on their heads, but it didn't. Something toppled to the floor. The cane tapped the linoleum and rolled in a semicircle. They could hear the house groaning as wind whistled in through the front doorway.

Brian whimpered.

The dragging and thumping started up again, going in the opposite direction now, down the length of the house. They heard the bathroom door get knocked open. They heard the curtains rattling as they were shoved aside. They heard the mirror break, shards screaming into the sink. It progressed into the master bedroom at the end of the hall. They heard knickknacks pelt the wall. A dresser crashed to the floor. A bed rolled out of its frame. A glass object burst.

The children huddled together under a table that was pushed against a shelving unit. The shelf was all that stood between them and the staircase.

Brian whispered, "Guest rooms."

Hannah shook her head. "No!"

"We can hide in there."

"No." Her brother started to crawl around the shelving unit. Hannah reached out and grabbed his ankle. "Brian."

"Give me these." Brian took their drinks away, holding them by their handles. "Let go. I don't wanna spill these."

"Brian!" Hannah's voice broke. She

321

was beginning to panic.

"Hurry!"

Hannah pursed her lips tightly. She let go and watched her brother take off like a jackrabbit with their mugs past the staircase, spilling tea and hot chocolate on the carpet. He disappeared into the first guest room. Hannah heard the mugs touch the surface of a desk or bedside table.

The basement door flew open. A shadow fell on them. Droplets of a thick liquid sprayed the steps as the intruder gagged on her own blood. Her jaw hadn't healed yet.

Hannah and Alistair looked at each other in wide-eyed terror. Donna Anderson had found them. She couldn't see them behind the shelving unit, but she didn't have to. She saw the spills on the stairs.

Hannah stole one final, desperate glance at the guest rooms. She couldn't see Brian in either of their dark doorways. She immediately regretted staying here behind the shelf. So stupid. It wasn't very high. The table would only provide minimal cover. Donna only had to go around the shelf to see them hiding under it. Stupid. Stupid.

322

Brian peeked out of the first guest room and looked at the shadow on the stairs. He stepped quietly out and moved along the wall, then disappeared into the second guest room.

Donna Anderson pitched forward, tumbled down the stairs. With her broken ankle, it was the only way she could descend unless she wanted to waste time leaning on the rail. She didn't feel any pain, so it was only a slight hindrance for her. She rolled down the last few steps and landed in a heap at the bottom, colliding with the shelving unit, shoving it inward on an angle. The shotgun clattered down the steps after her and thudded softly on the carpet. Hannah and Alistair hugged the floor under the table, covering their mouths. Waiting for the end. Praying it wouldn't hurt.

Donna untangled herself. She gripped the edge of the shelving unit to lift herself back on her good foot. She coughed blood and phlegm over the shelving unit, splattering the top of it, the table, and the carpet. She looked down.

Fresh stains in the carpet. Tea and hot chocolate. They were wet and warm.

323

She smelled the mixed aromas lingering in the air and limped toward the first guest room, dragging her bad foot across the carpet. She paused long enough to peer into the spare restroom. Then she disappeared into the guest room.

Brian bolted out of the second guest room, darted silently across the carpet, passing the first guest room, and rolled behind the shelving unit just as Donna Anderson emerged from the dark doorway. She'd heard something. She scanned the basement with narrow eyes. She checked the spare restroom more thoroughly, and then turned, limped into the second guest bedroom.

Brian signalled for them to follow his lead. He crawled on all fours up the steps. Hannah took Alistair's hand and pulled. He resisted. Hannah glanced back at him, begging him silently, desperately. He gave in, and as Hannah pulled him around the shelving unit, he watched that second doorway at the far end of the room. They crawled up the stairs. He heard the second guest room's temporary occupant cough up more blood and phlegm. Some of it splashed on the doorframe as she exited.

She looked at the stairs.

The children kept their strides light and wide as they progressed down the hall. Brian froze when he saw Sarah sprawled in the entryway to the kitchen with a massive chest cavity. Hannah prodded him to keep moving. They entered the foyer and saw the door had been blown inward off its hinges and now lay askew on the floor and a coat rack. They stepped around the door. Grabbed their boots. Carried them outside onto the doorstep. Alistair looked back and saw Harold slumped with his feet apart, his back against the lower cupboards. The contents of his head caked the cream-coloured cabinets. Strings of blood dribbled to the floor. The left side of his head was gone. His mouth hung open in a silent scream. His right eye watched the children leave.

Outside, their feet touched cold pavement. They slipped into their boots. Didn't bother tying the laces or doing up the Velcro straps. They took off down the path and up the driveway to the road. When they reached the road, they ran for town, pumping their little legs past trees and occasionally other houses. They didn't want to take their chances with another house. They cried as they ran, and they didn't stop until the sun peeked out from behind the trees, saturating the backroad in warm orange. Blankets of snow glimmered magically under dawn's new light all around them.

"With light comes the absence of monsters," Alistair recalled his mother saying. Night lights warded off dream demons. They would stay in the shadows, waiting for the night light to burn out, but they could never touch it, and it would never die. This angered them. Sometimes they would send nightmares to scare their would-be victims into making mistakes. People made mistakes when they were afraid. But the light would always protect Alistair, who always slept in its comforting glow. The demons could never touch him no matter how many nightmares they sent.

The woman was long gone. He looked back constantly as they progressed down the road and never saw her. Not once.

Their hearts felt like they were going to explode.

"Stop," Brian gasped, collapsing on

326

his knees. He wheezed heavily, trying to catch his breath. "I have... to stop!"

"Come on," Hannah panted, "we're almost there."

"No, we're not!" Brian retorted. "It's too far! We're not gonna make it."

Alistair, breathing hard, said, "I can't see her. She's not following us."

The children stood alongside each other and peered down the long stretch of road, shielding their eyes from golden rays of sunlight stabbing through the trees. They couldn't see her. The road was empty save for a little green dot of shimmering glass and metal. A faraway car approached.

"Maybe we can hitch a ride into town," Alistair thought aloud.

The siblings exchanged weary looks.

"What if she's driving that old couple's car?" Hannah asked.

Brian replied, "I didn't see one."

"They had a garage."

"Oh, yeah."

Alistair watched the car. It was still so far off that it appeared to be motionless. His cousins' words filled him with a sense of dread. *What if...?*

"Maybe we should hide," he said, and

327

before either of his cousins could respond, the trees across the ditch erupted with a horrible crash that resounded through the forest and sent flocks of frightened birds to seek refuge in the clouds.

A giant red spider lily bloomed from the side of Brian's head, its crimson petals shooting up into the sky as three sides of his stunned expression folded in opposite directions. His arms traced slow, lazy arcs around him as his legs wobbled. He twirled, sluggishly, as the contents of his ruptured head sprayed across the road. His body followed it, pivoting oddly. He landed flat on his back with his arms out, forming a crimson angel in a fresh blanket of previously undisturbed snow.

Hannah and Alistair stared at Brian's corpse, uncomprehending. The gunshot had shocked them into confused silence. The sight of Brian dying before their eyes felt like something straight out of a surreal nightmare. It couldn't be real. It had to be a nightmare. It *had* to be.

Hannah was the first to react to the sight of her dead brother—with a shrill scream. *"BRRIIIIIAAAAAAAANNN!"*

Alistair stared, his jaw hanging slack.

328

They heard that same throaty, gurgling cough behind them. Heard the splash of warm blood on frozen ditch water. They heard branches snapping, frozen leaves crunching under bare feet, ice breaking, and water sloshing as something shuffled through the ditch toward them. They turned and saw her. Her skin was as white as the snow she staggered through, a canvas for the macabre modern-art butterflies realized with careless strokes of brown and red paint. Her tongue flicked at them, still dangling loosely as a fleshy pink necktie. She vomited more blood. Streams of it poured off of her tongue. She inhaled, hissing loudly through her gaping throat in the back of her nonexistent mouth.

The children were frozen with fear, their nerves and instincts screaming for them to run, to cry, to check Brian and see if he was okay, if they were just seeing things, if this was all just a horrible dream. Their bodies refused all commands. They couldn't move under Donna's evil gaze. It was the only word anyone could describe the look she was giving them. It was unlike anything they had ever seen in anyone's— or anything's—eyes. Hungry, delighted,

329

unbridled evil.

Donna raised Dan Snr's shotgun. This time it was pointed at Alistair, who instinctively sucked in his last breath. She pulled the trigger. An empty chamber clicked.

It may as well have been the report of a starting pistol. The kids snapped into a full-tilt retreat for the faraway car. Their boots packing down snow faster than they thought possible, Hannah and Alistair left Brian behind. There was nothing they could do for him, now. Survival was all that mattered.

Donna Anderson was gaining despite dragging her foot behind her in a rapid, desperate limp. Crimson mist spewed from her gullet with every laboured breath as she bore down on them. She flailed her arm over her head and hurled the empty shotgun at them. It twirled between them and smacked the ground by Alistair's feet.

They didn't look back. Her hissing, bubbling gasps were getting closer. Her ankle was stripped to the bone from being dragged so far.

She was ten yards and gaining.

Hannah and Alistair ran in blind

330

panic, waving their arms out at the approaching car.

"Help! Help us!"

"Please help us!"

The car swerved to avoid the children, sliding on ice. A flurry of snow sprayed the trees as the car's rear tires spun over the top of the ditch. The driver fought the wheel. The car fishtailed along the ditch and then swung around to face the direction it came from.

Hannah reached the back door first, threw it open and dove inside. Alistair followed just as Donna descended on them. She took hold of his right ankle and dragged him back out of the car, but Hannah lurched forward and took his hand in both of hers. "Hannaaahhh!"

"Al!"

"Jesus!" the driver screamed. "Jesus Christ!" He floored the accelerator.

Alistair's tearful eyes bulged. He bellowed a feral shriek of terror, voice breaking, as he slid further out of the back seat, pulling Hannah with him. "HANNAH! HANNAAHH!"

Hannah saw that he was kicking desperately in an attempt to pry Donna

331

loose. She braced her feet against the sides of the doorway and pulled on both of his arms with all she had just as the car charged forward, dragging Alistair and Donna down the road and nearly yanking Hannah out with them.

The road tore Donna free from her prey with Alistair's boot in her hands. The inertia sent her tumbling after them and then skidding to a gradual stop.

Hannah heaved her cousin back into the car and held him tight against her, crying, laughing with maniacal relief as she watched Donna Anderson shrink into the distance in the rear window. The child was squealing incomprehensibly while the driver checked the mirrors on a constant basis. Alistair buried his face in his cousin's chest, sobbing quietly. He could feel the package under her coat.

*

The road was quiet, now. No birds sang. There was no wind to disturb the trees. Rabbits and deer were nowhere to be seen. It took Donna Anderson, now covered in fresh scrapes and bleeding gashes from the road, almost an hour to return to Brian's body. Half of what remained of her face had been severely avulsed courtesy of the frozen blacktop, with her eye bulging from a well of swelling, subcutaneous flesh that was beginning to freeze over. Her ear on the same side flapped loosely next to her tongue. Her fingers and smashed toes were black with frostbite.

She stood over Brian's body, casting a shadow over it. She coughed, splashing the corpse with bloody phlegm. She stooped down, curled her long, blackened fingers around one of Brian's legs, and dragged him off the road.

Into the ditch.

Into the forest.

To feed. And regain her strength.

Pink smears trailing off the road were left in her wake. A breeze whistled and tittered through wooden chimes dangling somewhere in the dense forest. They sounded like half a dozen train horns howling. The trees were alive with their call, whispering to each other until the wind died down. Then all was silent once again.

THE LAUGHTER IN THE WOODS

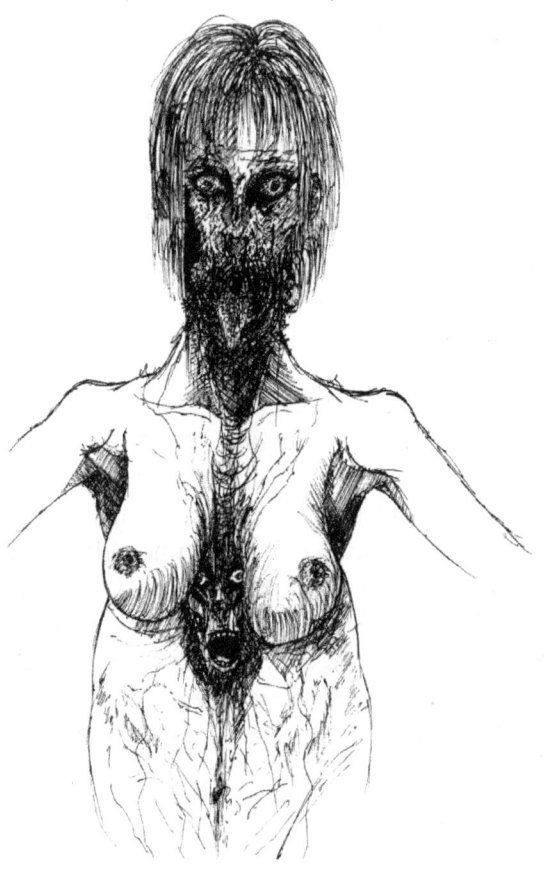

334

AFTERWORD

This is the third installment in what I'm calling the *Coldwater Tapes*, but chronologically, it's much farther ahead. Why did I skip over the timeline to write this one? Same reason I wrote *Bodycam*, which takes place in the same township as this and *She Watches Me Bury Her*, the latter taking place between *Bodycam* and this. So far, in chronological order, *Bodycam* comes first, though one doesn't necessarily need to read these in any specific order. I've been writing them to be enigmatic whether you've read one or two or none of them no matter the order. Is that the only reason they're enigmatic? For the sake of providing myself with the freedom to write these in whatever order I wish? Yes and no. There are a number of other reasons why I'm writing these loosely connected pieces out of order—none of which I'm going to tell you (LOL).

This is inspired by slashers,

335

psychological horrors, analog horror web series, and campfire stories. I think I originally conceived this from what little I could remember from an old nightmare. I remember when I was a kid, my paternal grandmother had a really nice house in the woods (not in like, dense, DENSE middle-of-nowhere woods, just on the outskirts of Coldwater in Oro-Medonte, Ontario), and my father would take my brother and I over there to celebrate Christmas. Our Oma Willi would always host family get-togethers at Christmastime, and while I have many fond memories of those, I do remember, when I was smaller, that once night started to fall, I'd feel a sense of dread.

I was a very superstitious child. I was afraid of the dark—it was so bad that I couldn't even go to the bathroom without waking my brother so that he'd walk me through the hall to the door. My imagination was growing more vivid, inspired by whatever crap I'd be watching on TV and reading in books. And, once night fell, I'd often look out the dining room window, over the deck, at the garden and the fish ponds scattered around the

336

trunks of maple trees and other brush. All those shifting leaves appeared to be shaping into other things. Things I didn't want to think about. It was as if the entire house was surrounded by some malevolent darkness that would close in on the place. And following my anxiety and wish to leave for the safety of my own home (despite the fact that those get-togethers were never dysfunctional in the slightest), the nightmares would come.

Obviously, I was bullshitting myself. What imaginative six-year-old isn't? The point is that it affected me on something of a primal level, and now it's manifested on paper for everyone else to enjoy. If 'enjoy' is really the right word to use...

This is a story that has taken years to make. I'm not entirely sure why, but I've found myself going back to older stories lately, ever since the completion of *Death Under Candyland's Eye*, a novel borne from a short about gangsters and undercover cops shooting each other up in a donut shop robbery gone wrong. I'd written that one action scene, which I thought was brilliant, personally, but no matter what I thought up, I just couldn't create a cohesive storyline around it until about eight years later. Now it's an 800-page novel totalling around 143,000 words, set to be published sometime in the summer of 2023. I feel like it may be some of my best work (so far) and the first book I've written that takes place in current events (at the time it was written, which is somewhere between summer of 2020 to spring of 2021). It features cover artwork by Ariel Zucker-Brull, an artist I've greatly admired for some time, and I will be commissioning more covers from him in the future. I'll still be designing my own, as well, as my own skills improve.

But anyways, back to *Laughter in the Woods*. About eleven years ago, I wrote a very short, very clumsy little yarn back when I was an amateur writer/artist on DeviantART, before I found out DeviantART can use your art for their own purposes without paying you for it. The short was very basic, and was more paranormal with none of the technological dread you see in this final form.

To sum it up, a brief family get-together is interrupted by an intruder in the yard, who laughs maniacally and hides

338

again every time he's seen. The family members quickly realize he isn't going away as he continues to approach the house from different hiding places in the surrounding woods. Eventually, the protagonist chases after him, but quickly loses sight of him. He spots footprints that lead back to the house. He follows them, and when he gets inside, the entire family has been turned into the same laughing shadows he's been chasing. Overcome with dread and grief, he opts to commit suicide before he can be turned into one of them.

It's a very bleak seven- or eight-page story, but it stayed in my mind more than ten years after I submitted it to DA. There are a few stories on there that I'll have another go at later on; I remember some of them, like an old Slender Man fan fiction (back when that was a thing) I had told in about nine parts called *Slendy* and *Catching Slendy*, in which children befriend a creature who lures them into the nearby woods. This one is actually going to be the basis for a future *Coldwater Tapes* story, called *Sleepless Children*. Not sure how many of these I'll write, as I have a few ideas for future installments, but I may cap it off at six. Seems like a good number.

I'm also interested in revisiting another old story, this one a stand-alone called *Cries in the Night*, which involved a classic noir-style detective hunting a killer whose M.O. is similar to that of the banshee. There are a few others I'd like to revisit, but I won't get into those right now.

At the moment, I'm working a lot of hours at my job, drawing as much as I can, and writing as much good material as can be salvaged. I'd hoped to publish this and *BRITTLE FIST* sooner in the year, but life had other plans, I guess. *BRITTLE FIST* will be my first publication of 2023, a novella about a man transformed by vengeful rage against a man who has overcome a similar ordeal, leading up to a brutal confrontation between them that could destroy the world. It's an uncompromising nightmare that is heavily inspired by Japanese cyberpunk, body horror, and industrial/techno metal.

After that, I'll be focusing mainly on getting future *Cobalt Rogue* volumes out. Currently working on *Vol. 4: Cemetery Rumble, Part II* and its second half, *Vol.*

4.5: Renegade's Revenge, both of which I'm very excited for. A lot of the crazy things I've envisioned for the *Cobalt Rogue* series will be occurring in these two volumes.

It's just a matter of keeping myself from getting distracted by movies, video games, and YouTube. Wish me luck.

And stay tuned.

-2022

<u>Works by Alexander Engel-Hodgkinson</u>

Clockworld (One-Shot)
I Keep My True Love in the Basement (One-Shot)
Reality Glitch ('Jumping for Charlotte' segment)
No Bounds ('Cranston & Layman' segment)
BRITTLE FIST*

<u>The Final Apocalypse Saga</u>
(IN CHRONOLOGICAL ORDER)

Vol. 1: The Dead Blue
Vol. 2: Sky Japan Welcome Party
Vol. 3: Cemetery Rumble, Part I
Vol. 3.5: Hell Week
Vol. 4: Cemetery Rumble, Part II*
Vol. 4.5: Renegade's Revenge*
Vol. 5: Cemetery Rumble, Part III*
Post-Apocalyptic Days
Cobalt Christmas
I Keep My True Love in the Basement/REMIX

<u>ZYKLON IV Continuum</u>
(IN CHRONOLOGICAL ORDER)

Bodycam
She Watches Me Bury Her
The Laughter in the Woods
The Tea Party Affair
Jumping for Charlotte
Death Under Candyland's Eye*

*coming soon